Twilight Time

By the Same Author

My Elvis Blackout
Monkey's Birthday

Twilight Time

Simon Crump

BLOOMSBURY

First published in Great Britain by Bloomsbury Publishing Plc 2004
This paperback edition published 2006

Copyright © 2004 by Simon Crump

Bloomsbury Publishing Plc, 36 Soho Square, London W1D 3QY

A CIP catalogue record for this book
is available from the British Library

ISBN 0 7475 8181 9
9780747581819

Typeset by Hewer Text Ltd, Edinburgh
Printed in Great Britain by Clays Ltd, St Ives plc

All papers used by Bloomsbury Publishing are natural, recyclable
products made from wood grown in well-managed forests.
The manufacturing processes conform to the environmental
regulations of the country of origin.

www.bloomsbury.com/simoncrump

Acknowledgements

Thanks to Lorraine Butler, Nell Farrell, Jane Roughley, Rennie Sparks, Victoria Hobbs, Mary Tomlinson, Duncan McLean, Bryan Franklin, Dave Woodhouse, Mick Jones, Mike Jones, Ann & Brian.

Apologies to Philip Larkin.

For Lorraine

His hands might have trembled. He wondered what would happen if he pissed his pants. And did let go one little spurt. At once his fear took on a shape: if he had had a pencil in his hand he would have drawn Death trumpeting.

He felt better after that.

Patrick White, *The Vivisector*

Bruno trots in front of me on a slack leash. He pulls up at the first drain we get to, splays his hind legs, lifts his tail and squats.

'That's the boy,' I tell him, and his watery brown eyes meet mine.

'There's a boy.'

Six times out of ten they fall. Through the cast-iron grid, out of sight and out of my jurisdiction, which is exactly the way I like it, and exactly the way most things are these days. Way out of my jurisdiction.

Not this morning, though. I dip into the pocket of my Thornproof and fish out a Safeway sandwich bag. I slip the bag over my right hand and grasp the turd, a thin layer of polythene between cold flesh and warm brown jobby. I bag it, tie it, double-bag it, knot it and pocket it.

We pass the bus stop and the usual gaggle of teenagers. Young lads in sports gear fagging away and lasses showing far too much leg and for their age a fair amount of tit.

Same as always the runt kicks off.

'Eee fuckin' 'ell, it's fuckin' lovejoy,' he shrieks. 'Sold any clocks today, mester, shagged any old ladies?'

Bruno starts to growl. I let him off the lead and he goes charging over. Next minute he's squirming on his back. The runt's tickling his tummy and I'm stood there like a cunt.

A cunt with a bag of shit going cold in his pocket.

I hate that fucking dog. First pick of the litter and I chose the poof.

Bruno settles in his box by the radiator, curls into himself and sleeps – lucky little bastard. I make myself a quick coffee then roll and smoke first fag of the day – the obligatory laxative roll-up. I make a mug of tea for Linda so I can combine the trip upstairs with the toilet.

I knock on Linda's bedroom door.

'Come,' she says.

'Chance'd be a fine thing,' I say under my breath.

I set the tea on her bedside table and same as every morning it steams over the photo of our wedding day. Me handsome in my uniform, Linda trussed up in her mother's dress, all nipples and organza, thick fog drifting in.

When I wed her she was smashing. Tits to die for and a big round arse – definitely a lady with the fuller figure – but ripe and lovely and mine, all mine. Christ Jesus, look at her now. Propped up in her single bed, frilly blue nightie, a pint of menopausal perspiration in her pants and the first of today's instructions forming on her lips.

That cow makes me sick. And I can't believe, I can't believe I ever wanted to shag that, or even anything that big. Not in a month, not in a year of fucking Sundays.

Two years into the marriage Linda's eyes went. She won't wear contacts. Truth be told they probably can't make them that thick.

Linda wears expensive specs. Dennis Taylor-made upside-down snooker loopy owlface giglamps, the lenses so thick they magnify her eyes to pickled eggs.

Her body was never really the same after carrying Richard. Her hair is something else and there's no good reason for that.

'Morning, Linda, drop your cock and grab your socks, it's eight-thirty.'

'Two things, Bruce,' she squeaks. 'One, we're neither of us in the army any more and two, we didn't have cocks in my battalion.'

'Sorry, dear, how about drop your rat and grab your hat. Is that any better?'

'No, Bruce, it is not. It isn't nice when you talk like that and you'd better mind your ps and qs today and specially your fs and cs, we've got Richard – the new long-term volunteer – starting, so let's make sure this one really is long-term, shall we, please? He'll be here at ten so you'd better get on . . . and don't forget your tablets.'

'No, dear, I won't, soon as I get downstairs I'll take them,' I say, backing away.

'Oh Brucie,' she giggles, turning up her cheek. 'Aren't you forgetting something, my big brave sergeant?'

Same as every morning I don't much fancy it, but I lean over to kiss her anyway. She grabs the back of my neck, forces my head down into her sweaty cleavage and strokes my hair, and same as every morning she whispers something saucy in my ear.

'Finish your chores double quick, soldier, then meet me behind the guardhouse – it'll only cost you a fiver.'

That's the girl. Same as every morning I feel the loose flesh of her breasts snag up in my smile and same as every morning I fall in love all over again and feel it stirring. Same as every morning it fades away.

God forgive me, Lindy, you're still gorgeous to me.

S ame as every morning I start the chores and same as every morning I wonder how the hell this happened. Linda in charge and me cleaning the fucking bogs, but I pull my tan one-piece overall up over my green elephant cords and button the front. I leave the top two unlatched so you can still see the cravat. It's smart to be smart and as Linda always says it's nice to be nice. It doesn't hurt to look smart even if you can't be nice and even if you are only cleaning the bogs.

I take the galvanised-metal bucket from under the sink in the volunteers' kitchen, add a capful of Dettol, watch the water cloud white and fetch a mop from down the side of the filing cabinet where Linda keeps the visitor information packs.

I always think that mop looks a lot like Linda except it's thinner. She says her hair's a bob but it's always struck me as more of a moptop. John, Paul, George, Ringo and Linda. Sexiest man in my platoon and I married moptop number five from outer space. I fill the bucket two-thirds to the top with hot water, then dip in Linda's head and do the floor. The room fills with the smell of disinfectant, the same stuff they use to blot out the waft of school dinners and the stench of terminal illness.

It's the oldest chestnut in the oldest book but school-days really were the happiest of my life. No problem with girls, no problem with clothes, and no problem and no chance of thinking for myself.

Big School. Boys and masters, masters and boys. Day one, term one they gave you a timetable.

You stuck it in your inside pocket and you stuck to it. Pink card reinforced with open-weave linen folded three times into itself.

Monday to Saturday – lessons, private study and prep. Blocked out in block capitals. Forty-five-minute periods, ninety-minute doubles.

On the front the phoney school crest, on the back religious holidays, sporting fixtures, notes on the royals and lines from Shakespeare. Did you know the Queen Mother was President of the British Colostomy Society? And if you did do you really give a fuck? I thought not.

We assembled in tower-block room T2. Neddy stood behind the lectern and flicked back his pedal-bin haircut. All that thing really required was a fucking chinstrap. Neddy flicked it back anyway and frightened us with a yard of rubber tubing while we filled the calendar in.

Day one, year two they did it again. The calendar. Different shade of card this time but the details and fixtures the same and it stayed like that for the next five years. They'd tell you when to speak and when to not, when and where to sit, when to shit and when to pretend to relax. You're batting on the O level wicket now, my fine young gentleman: keep your eye on the ball and don't let the side down.

We did English, O level lit. Literature. And I liked that, all those books, all those things people had sat down and written, all those words bursting off the page. The English man, the man who taught English, Hopkins I think his name was, had the shiniest shoes I've ever seen. He took us to his house once, for revision. Books all up the stairs and a bicycle in the kitchen. Larkin, the most miserable fucker in the whole wide world, Shakespeare and First World War poetry. And Faulkner. My mother is a fish. I remember that. My mother is a fish.

I remember the eleven-plus very clearly and for all the wrong reasons. Mountford Primary. Me and a pal called Sim Lister, a barefoot curly kid whose parents' garden was filled with twisted metal sculpture, followed Susan Trevor into the woods and she finally agreed to what we'd been egging her to do for weeks. Half a dozen penny snakes and a blackjack sealed the deal.

We'd show her ours if she showed us hers.

'Girls go first,' says Sim, so Susan pulls her broad navy pants down around her knees. Me and Sim kneel. We look at her little red rat, then at each other, then at her little red rat again. Our turn now.

We don't stop running till stitch staples our guts at the edge of the staff car park. Sim leans over Miss

Keeble's smart new Morris and catches his breath. I fall against Mr Timpson's rusty old Oxford and do the same. I straighten up, look over at Sim and realise that he's crying.

'It looked like beetroot,' he sobs over and over, 'it just looked like beetroot.'

The bell rings. We go inside, hang up our coats, satchels, then file into assembly.

Mr Timpson plays us 'Hard Day's Night' on the school Dansette, a record which even at our tender age we know is all about shagging, but he talks about it after and bends it round to God.

We sing a hymn, then Tania Gartshore, brainiest, poshest and pig-ugliest girl in the school, takes to the lectern and makes us have the bit from the Bible about Jesus going out into the desert where for forty days and nights he got tempted by Satan.

Only she stumbles over desert and it comes out dessert so instead of the son of God sweating his bollocks off in a hot sandy place for forty days and nights you get a picture of big J. up to his armpits in his mum's best sherry trifle with the Devil tormenting him: 'Go on, pal, it's day thirty-nine, one tiny spoonful's not going to hurt you, well, is it now?'

The reading ends then Timpo announces, 'All fourth-year to stay behind after, please. Everybody else may go. Good morning, children.'

'Good morning, Mr Timpson.'

And so years one, two and three file out. I'm looking at Sim and his face is all pink and puffy and I'm thinking surely Susan can't have ratted on us for not keeping our half of the deal, seeing as she got the sweets and everything, and then we're both looking at Roderick Mulchay who pinches his old man's Players and hands you out a numbo if you give him the money, then at Wayne who pissed in Helen Brown's pencil case, then Kevin Shelton who shat up the side of Miss Keeble's car and then on the same day got binned out of the choir for trying to sing 'Move It' to the tune of 'All Things Bright and Beautiful', and it settles on me that it's the whole year.

They're keeping us all back and there must be a reason, and I think that maybe somebody's died again. Oh Christ. A week last Tuesday poor Michael Yeomans from Outwards Road sneaks into assembly ten minutes late. Timpson spots him and in front of the whole school Michael gets the third degree.

'Why are you late this morning, Michael?'

'Me mummy's dead.'

'That is such a wicked lie,' says Timpo. 'I saw your mother only yesterday. She picked you up after school.'

'When I came down this morning,' says Michael, 'she had her head on the table and when I went to wake her she fell on the floor. I've checked and Mummy's not breathing.'

'Have you told anybody, Michael?'

'Yes, Mr Timpson sir, I've just told you.'

But it's not that this morning. Nobody's dead, not yet at any rate.

The caretaker comes in and he takes care. Him and the PE man start laying out the tables all ready for school dinners, but they don't set them up the same as usual – eight little ones to make a big block – they set 'em up singly with a metal-framed canvas stacking chair hard up behind each one. Miss Keeble flaps a stapled wad on to each desk and Timpo lines us up.

Miss Keeble moves down the line with a brand-new box of pencils like a conjurer at a docile kids' party. She tells us to pick a chair, any chair.

This must be an exam, a test they've not told us about.

I sit right at the front and examine my smart new pencil. Royal-blue, six sides, a pink eraser bound to its blunt end by a narrow tin band. It's been sharpened so recently it smells like a tree again. It's perfect.

The point's too sharp. I just know it'll break. Soon as I start to write my name.

I stare at the pencil and I notice that the way it's been sharpened has cut dark-blue paint into the frilly scallops you see round the edge of a circus big top, then I jam the point of the pencil into one of the hollow silver rivets which fixes the tight red canvas to my chair's cream tubular frame and snap the end clean off the fucker.

That's more like it, I'm thinking. It would have happened anyway, it wouldn't have lasted. Best get it over and done with, eh?

Then I look up. Everyone's hunched over their desks

and they're all scribbling away like bastards. They've started without me.

So anyway that was it. I think that was it. That was when I went up to the front and asked for another pencil and Miss Keeble looked at what I'd done to the first one and tutted but she gave me a fresh one and didn't say anything, so it must have been important and I think that was it.

It was. And looking back I can't really remember what they asked us aged eleven, or what I put. Although I do remember doing a really good drawing of an avocet and writing a whole page about a sailing dinghy.

Two weeks before we finished at Mountford, Timpo held us back again and read out a list.

And I know now that he was being fair, or at least he thought he was, but he read out the names of the whole fourth year and after each boy's name he said 'Garendon' and after each girl's he said 'De Lisle'. And then he says there are two names missing from this list.

'Bruce Glasscock.'

Which is me – they called me brittledick in the army.

'And Ian Roper,' he booms. 'Well done, lads, you've got free places at the grammar.'

I look over at Ropey, he looks at me, and I wonder.

He's a really bright lad. He's got grade three clarinet and his brother lives in Norway. And then there's me.

The beetroot-researching boy who broke the pencil. We've both just won today's star prize and I know why Ropey has all right, but not me. And then I understand. They just gave it to the brightest kid in the class and the one with the funniest name.

Grammar doesn't start till mid-September so I've got thirteen weeks of unbroken leisure before I enter the great institution.

For the first, and definitely the last, time my folks are really proud.

So they get me a second-hand bike, a set of Kohinoor pencils and a new fishing rod.

That was such a miserable time. I looked forward to it so much but when it arrived it felt all wrong. An undeserved thirteen weeks' rest after winning an accidental Olympic gold and I began to worry that maybe they timed me when I ran away from Susan Trevor, maybe the adjudicators sponsored by Accurist were watching as I broke a record, then a pencil. Beat the all-comers under-elevens' time for running from a girl who showed me what I wanted to see. Or maybe, and more likely, it was a big fat mistake just waiting to be revealed.

To celebrate my triumph and in honour of my outstanding academic achievement Dad decided to spruce up the Hillman.

He bought a gallon of enamel and hired a gun for twenty-four hours. I can never remember the reg of that particular car but that day I danced around it in the road singing out the letters and numbers over and over while Dad hosed it end to end with charcoal-blue paint.

He resprayed the bodywork, the rusty chrome

bumpers, decaying mazack doorhandles and most of the red-vinyl upholstery, then we stood back to admire the job and watched as all the flies within a mile's radius instantly stuck themselves to it.

Andrew Goodacre roared past in his fifth-hand Austin, slewing gravel all up one side, then next door's red setter Fritz came out to see what all the swearing was about, joined in the fun and took a piss against the nearside passenger door.

You wouldn't think dog piss could blister a fresh coat of cellulose to quite that extent, but it does.

Dad grabbed his gun and went inside. He did the drawers of Mum's English rose kitchen and then for good measure he did my bike as well, and the toaster and the fridge and my mum's sewing machine and the back wall in the pantry, our dustbin and next door's dustbin – without asking them but he thought they'd like it to match – and then he did Cyril Atkin's caravan up the road, the rusty bottom half of Gran's Ford Anglia, the top of her breadbin, next-door-but-one's radiogram and then the fridge again as the white was showing through. He still had some paint left, so in desperation he did his gardening shoes and the first coat went orange peel. Dad wet and dried 'em and sprayed 'em up again.

That holiday dragged on for ever. Dad made me a little pond. I watched a perfect glistening baby frog sun itself too long, shrivel and die.

In July Dad smacked me and tore up all my drawings. In August he made me weed the rosebed and call him sir. Me glad and sorry all at once, not knowing why, not knowing what I'd done wrong, but afraid of being rumbled all the same. Then autumn nipping in and me still not back at school, Mum crying every time she laid a hand on me and me still not knowing why.

The letter came a week ago.

Linda ripped through the usual irrelevant directives from Trust HQ, the unhelpful penny-paring suggestions from regional office and a shirty reminder from Swift's that the fire extinguishers needed checking.

Then a neat handwritten A4 envelope – buff, polite and informal.

Inside a short chatty note from Richard offering his services, and a three-page CV.

'Blimey, Bruce,' she says. 'Have a look at this. Three pages! He's got a CV better than you and me put together and he's offering to work for free.'

'So what's wrong with him?' I say. 'There must be a catch, there always is. Always.'

'No, I don't think so, love,' she says. 'He's got a degree, an MA, he's taught in schools and colleges, he's even worked for a building society.'

'So why does he want to work for us? There has to be a catch.'

'He says that he came on a timed visit to the Hays a couple of weeks ago, that he's not wanting to work in education any more and wants to get involved in the Trust.'

'Well, he's welcome to it, penny-pinching ungrateful bunch of toffee-nosed bastards.'

'They're not that bad, Bruce. They gave me this job and us both a home. They even pay you for little bits of work.'

And I think yeah, that's about the size of it.

I've got a home which isn't mine, a wife who wears the trousers and little bits of work. I clean little bits of shit off the bogs, cut little bits of grass off the lawns, take the dog for little walks and swallow little white pills three times a day. That's me sorted then. Linda's little helper. Only Linda's going to have a brand-new, brainy, new little helper – a long-term volunteer, if you don't mind. He's been to college, he's done this, he's done that and I hate the fucker's guts already.

'I think I'll ring him now, Bruce, see if he can start first thing Monday next week. Can you reach me the phone?'

'Yes, dear.'

The doorbell went ten sharp.

Soon as I saw the kid I liked him, knew we'd get on fine. Smart black suit, lace-up dockers, open shirt, close-cropped hair.

Linda brought him through to the kitchen, we shook hands and after I'd finished with his mitt he made a joke about never being able to play the violin again. And you can see he's a bit shy, but there's a smile in his eyes and he's got proper manners. He's not making an effort to please or to thank you – he's just like that.

I like that and so does Linda. Christ, some of the others we've had. Spineless. Right ignorant sods and spotty and smelly too some of them. Never last very long.

Linda makes him a coffee – white no sugar – and he winces when I ask where mine is and she snaps back at me to make my own.

'We're very free and easy here, Richard, we don't stand on ceremony and you'll have to take us as you find us,' I say, covering up for the fact that he's been in the building for just over a minute and already Linda's made me look like a full-weight cunt.

We all settle round the kitchen table and you can tell that her snapping at me like that has made him nervous. His hands are shaking slightly – not enough for Linda to notice – but I spot it straight off. It all feels a bit tense and he's staring at a blob of jam on the table left over from breakfast. I don't know what to say or really what I should be doing, so I do what I always do when it gets like this. I fish out my Golden Virginia, my green Rizla packet and my box of Swan, and I start rolling a fag.

'It's OK to smoke?' Richard asks.

'I don't see why not,' says Linda. 'Bruce does all the time, but only in here, never next door and not even in here if we have anybody down from regional HQ.'

'Brilliant. Thank fuck for that, sorry, thank goodness for that.' He laughs, and coming from him and the way he says it, the f word sounds OK. It sounds like quite a nice posh word in fact and I can see from Linda's face she hasn't even registered it. She'd have shouted at me by now.

Richard produces a pack of Golden Virgina, the same green papers as me, and does the same. 'Look,' Linda says, 'a hand-roller just like you, Bruce.'

'Not many of us left these days,' he says and the atmosphere lifts.

It's the us that does it. Us, as in us smokers. Us, as in our little gang. Us, as in the reason why I started smoking in the first place.

From day one in the woods behind the staff car park, us smoking Roderick's old man's numbos while our faces turned green, until now in the kitchen, me and a total stranger. I like us, I like it a lot. It's not often I get included in anything. Richard finishes rolling his fag and frowns as he slides open the box of Swan.

'Strewth,' he says in a fake Aussie accent, just like in the lager ad, 'don't you just hate it when that happens?' and he pushes the box across the table towards me.

'The girlfriend borrows 'em to light the barbie, well, the cooker really,' he says dropping the accent, 'and she always puts the dead ones back. Now that's all there is.'

I pick through the box just to see if I can prove him wrong but he's right. Every single one a darkie.

'All niggers in there, Richard, every last useless one,' I say. 'Tip 'em in the bin where they all belong.'

He laughs but his face changes. His eyes go stiff and he looks embarrassed.

I lean across the table to spark him up and as I take the match away my hand brushes his hand.

'Cheers, Bruce,' he says, 'thanks very much, very decent of you, old man,' and he's the first ever volunteer who's ever had the guts to take the rise out of the way I speak and I laugh and Linda laughs and she grins at me and me and Richard smoke a fag and it's OK. We share the moment and it's OK.

Linda takes Richard through the routine. The schedule, the bookings and the timed visits. It's nearly the end of the season so we've only got a fortnight of brainless rubbernecking scum to put up with before we put the house to bed for the winter and make a start on what Linda calls the real work.

'I think we'll start you off in the exhibition room, Richard,' she says. And I like the 'we'. That really makes me laugh. That's not 'we' as in Linda and me, Bruce and Linda the happy couple, oh no, that's 'we' as in the royal 'we'. She doesn't half love somebody new to boss around does my Lindy.

'That's the room first left off the hall, which should be the best room, it's where we show the visitors their pre-tour video of the house. Second on the left, the back parlour, is my office. Apart from this kitchen me and Bruce live upstairs – it's a big enough house for that. We've still got two floors up there – which is plenty for us – and it gives us a bit more privacy.

'If you want to sit in with me for this morning and then take over in the afternoon – if you feel confident enough – that'd be great. I've got loads of paperwork to catch up on.'

'Yeah,' he says, 'OK. But if you are dead busy and you don't mind, I'll just start this morning. You can sit in with me for a bit to check if you want, but I'll not be making a mess of it. I'll be fine, honestly.'

I roll my eyes at Linda and I'm thinking cocky little bastard, he's only been here five minutes and already he's Mr Ex-fucking-pert and Linda looks a bit surprised, well, a lot surprised actually, and she gives me an old-fashioned look.

'No, really,' he says, 'I can see what you're thinking, but I'm not being funny or anything. You probably think it's dead cocky and that, but I do know what to do. I did come on a visit so I've seen it done and I have taught in all sorts of terrible places and like they say most teaching is a cross between crowd control and showbiz anyway, and I am trying to impress you and make you think that I'm great, well obviously, but I reckon I can do it OK.

'If you want to check, that'll be fine, but I thought I was supposed to be here to help you out. There is loads of stuff I want to learn, which you will need to teach me – the conservation stuff and that, but not this, this bit, well, it's what I'm used to.'

'So how are you going to do it then, Richard?' Linda asks him sounding stern, overpolite, and from where I'm standing, rip-your-bollocks-off snippy.

'Well,' he says, sounding less confident by the second. 'I show the visitors in, I get them sat down and I welcome them to the Hays House, then I tell them a bit about William and Walter Hays and put the video on.

'We watch that and then I show them back down the path they've all just come up, then up next door's path and introduce them to whoever's showing them round the Hays House. That's it, isn't it?'

'So what about the money?' Linda asks him.

'The money? I don't think we paid when we came, I thought it was all free here – like a charity thing.'

'No,' she says. 'No. It most certainly is not free. There's life members, associate members, family members, group rates, discounts with tokens from magazines, then concessions for children, students and OAPs. So how come you never paid anyway? Who was on the day you came?'

Richard gives me a look, and I realise that he knows it was me and I know that he knows and I remember exactly why I forgot to charge him and his stubby little mate and the two gorgeous girls they came with and why I fumbled over the lines and on three separate occasions called the offshot kitchen the offshit kitchen, and why the till was so badly down that Linda said I couldn't be trusted ever to do it again. But I can see he's not going to let on, and I swing from hating the cunt to thinking he's a smashing young chap all over again.

'Er, I dunno, Linda,' he says. 'I can't really remember. We came in a bit late and we thought it was free anyway, so we never thought to ask how much it was to get in, and I think the bloke, the lady who was on, a, er, short lady with hair, long darkish hair, probably was so busy that he, er, she, forgot to ask us.'

'So you don't know about the charges, Richard, and can you operate a till, manage a float and balance up at the end of the day? And what about when they come back in again after the timed visit wanting to buy postcards and guidebooks and souvenir pencils? Do you know the prices of those and how to keep track of the stock?'

'Shit. No,' he says, and that's the second time he's done that and the second time Linda hasn't noticed and the second time he's got away with it. 'You know how some people are with words, they see a sign "Guard Dogs On Patrol" and they read "Free Dog With Petrol"? Dyslexic they call it, well, that's how I am with numbers. I see a column of figures and I feel like crying. I just panic and feel like crying. Look, Linda,' Richard says, 'I'm sorry,' and lays his head on the table.

He flops his hand down on the melamine like a useless flipper and shoves the big cut-glass ashtray towards her.

'Hit me,' he says, pointing to the back of his head. 'Hit me there with that. I'm really sorry. Can we forget I said any of that? I'm just not fit for anything. I'm meant to be here to make your life easier. I've only been here five minutes and I'm rubbish, not fit for proper work. I'll clean the bogs instead.'

I've never seen anything like it. I've been married to Lindy nigh on twenty-five years and I swear I've never seen it before or since. Linda starts breathing hard, only for a few seconds, mind, and then every bit of flesh you can see of her, from her ankles to her wrists to the base of her cleavage to her neck to her face to the tiny patch of flesh you can see through the crown of her alien moptop goes bright scarlet and then this noise starts coming out of her, and I'm starting to think she's having some kind of fit and then it turns into a laugh, a mechanical seaside sailor hysterical laugh that goes on for about five minutes.

Lindy takes a drink straight off the cold tap – which

I've never seen her do in company before – then staggers over to me and Richard and throws her arms around our necks and clutches us to her bosom – which is nice for me but probably less so for Richard.

'Oh my brave boys,' she chokes, the tears and the sweat streaming down her puffy pink face. 'What on earth am I going to do with you two?'

First of today's timed visits is booked in for eleven-thirty.

Five twittering tarts from the bowls club. And I can picture it now. They'll be wearing their Sunday best and they'll all have had their hair done special. Crash-helmet perms every last one of them. And they'll stink. Talc, deodorant and just a hint of Persil. They'll sit in the exhibition room and not listen to the tape. Then they'll flutter round the house oohing and aahing and making stupid chicken noises at all the useless junk William and Walter packed into it during their mean-ingless lives and saying how their old mum used to have one just like that and I haven't seen one of those for years and wasn't everything nicer in the good old days?

Well, actually, ladies, no. It was not, not round here at any rate. Life in this little town was hard, short and for the most part shit.

Nearly forgot. Monday is bin day and Bin day is monday.

I drag the wheelie bin out of its hiding place behind the coal bunker – Trust rules say we have to keep it out of sight – and then down to the corner where our drive meets the main Gateford Road. I prop my elbows on top of the bin, roll a fag, spark it up and watch the traffic.

Usually I wait for the bin lorry. I like to have a word with the bin lads then wheel the wheelie bin straight home again.

Some of the flange those mucky, lucky lads get to see. The offers they've had. You wouldn't believe.

All along the Coleridge Drive frustrated middle-aged women in silk designer nighties bend over to fondle twin bottles of silver top and show off posh pointy breasts, every last one gagging for a bit of mid-morning rough.

Meanwhile on the Spungeon Estate, pert double rows of young unmarried mothers flaunt themselves in the rotting bay windows of identical maisonettes. Minges pulse inside a selection of earth's tautest and tiniest tanga briefs, with a nice pair of tits on special offer and a big dirty cock-guzzling smile thrown in for free – bored shitless and begging for it.

Wish I was a bin man.

These days the council calls its dustmen waste disposal operative teams – but that's a Sunday name.

The bin lads call themselves fanny patrol. Give 'em half a chance, ladies, and they'll slip inside your front porches and scuttle up your back passages double-quick time.

Wish I was a bin man. The pay's good, the job keeps you fit, you're out in the fresh air all morning and down the pub by dinner. You don't have to think or worry about fuck all.

Five minutes' training and you're in.

Pavement bin. Bin pavement. Bin to lorry. Bin lorry. Lorry bin. Full bin in cradle. Press red button. Up she goes. Empty bin. Bin empty. Press green button. Down she comes again. Replace empty bin on pavement a minimum of 200 yards away from correct house. Repeat as necessary and Robert's your father's brother. Got that, son? Good. One hat, dustman's for the use of. One pair corblimey trousers. One set keys to council flat.

Sign here. Sorry? No problem – put an x instead. Lovely. Welcome to fanny patrol.

Wish I was a bin man.

Can't stay this morning, much as I'd like to, it's time for my chores in the car park.

Just over the road from the house there's a square of shingle in the middle of William and Walter's old allotment and, every day before the first of the visitors arrive, I have to set up the A-frame sign which says 'Car Park'. I rake out the gravel and pick up the bits of litter – another one of my favourite little jobs. When I'm done I park the rake and as I walk up the path and past the front bay window I hear voices in the exhibition room.

I let myself in the back door and wash my hands in the kitchen sink. Linda's sat at the table with her big desk diary, planning out next year's volunteer rota.

'Where's laughing boy got to, Linda?'

'Sorry, Bruce?'

'Richard, where is he?'

'He's in the exhibition room. He's practising, said he wanted to check out the acoustics but I think that was a joke. He's made himself a chart and you should see it, Bruce. He's photocopied all the different tickets, the postcards and the guidebooks, even the pencils, on to a sheet of paper and he's written the prices down next to them and he's taped it under the counter. I've just shown him how to work the till. I said if he gets stuck just to keep a record of everything he sells and we'll sort it out later.

'So what do you think, Bruce?'

'What?'

'About Richard – what do you reckon?'

'Seems OK to me, cocky mind you, but nice enough. He made you laugh.'

I can't believe it. The cow actually asked my opinion. She never does that, she never includes me in anything to do with this house. In fact she usually goes right out her way to make sure I've got so little idea of what's going off that if I do say something I make an arse of myself and that's the way my Lindy likes it. Her in charge and me looking like a brainless twat.

There's a thud as something connects with our wheelie bin out on the corner of the Gateford Road. Me and Linda go into the hallway and peer through a clear bit of pattern in the etched-glass front door.

A powder-blue Volvo estate with its headlights on full beam crunches up the fractured tarmac of our unadopted road. It swings into the car park and performs an accidental wheelspin all across my newly raked gravel.

The ladies are here. They're overdressed, they're overexcited and they're early. They flutter across the road like a flock of geriatric parrots and the bossy one – there always is a bossy one – rings the doorbell.

Linda taps on the exhibition-room door and it opens a crack.

'They're here, Richard.'

'Oh shit,' he says under his breath and yet again Linda fails to register.

'Oh dear, oh no, oh no, no, no,' he cries in a fake hysterical voice.

'They're early. I've not rewound the tape. I'm not ready, I can't remember my name and I can't feel my legs. We're all doomed, doomed, I tell you,' and then he bursts out into the hallway grinning like a bag of cheese.

'Right, ready,' he says. 'Let me at 'em.'

'Are you sure you don't want me to sit in with you, Richard?'

'No way, Lindypoos,' he cackles. 'I'm totally in control.'

Me and Linda edge back down the hallway into shadow and lurk in the threshold of the door to the kitchen. Richard hauls open the front door.

'Good morning, ladies, and welcome to the Hays House. My name's Richard and I will be your steward for the next forty-five minutes. We will be flying at an altitude of approximately 5 feet and at an average speed of 200 miles per hour.

'The emergency exits are situated here – and here.'

He grins, motioning towards a matching pair of framed watercolour sketches of Shireoaks Priory.

'If you care to follow me and park your bums, I'll relieve you of your cash, any jewellery or other valuables you may have stashed about your persons, and then we'll all watch a film, no nudity or bad language, I'm afraid, but it is very informative and there's a really good car chase just before the end.'

The ladies are jammed into the hallway smiling and nudging each other and two old girls bringing up the rear have gone pink and are trying not to laugh.

'Do you think he's on drugs, Bruce?' Linda whispers. 'He just called me Lindypoos.'

'No, dear, I think he's maybe a little nervous, but he's very good, isn't he?'

'Right,' Richard says. 'Walk this way, ladies,' then he hunches up his shoulders and does a Douglas Bader, pretends his left leg has gone tin. He starts dragging himself towards the exhibition room and then he pauses.

'I'm terribly sorry,' he says in an RAF accent. 'I really am most awfully sorry. That was in extremely poor taste. Most of you lot probably walk like that anyway.'

And it's far too much for them. It's not what they'd expected but they don't mind that, not a bit. The ladies begin clutching at each other and a posh peal of laughter washes down the hallway. Richard ushers the ladies into the exhibition room and the door swings to. Just before it closes completely he sticks his head out into the hallway.

'OK?' he mouths at Linda.

'Yes, er, fine, Richard, but maybe tone it down just a tiny bit – we don't want any heart attacks, not on your first day.'

'Me or them? Yeah, anyway, sure, no problem', and the door snaps shut.

We hear the till going and the chink of money and more laughter.

'I feel like we're missing out here, Bruce.'

'Yes, I know what you mean, Lindypoos.'

She kicks my ankle and flounces off. I follow her into the office. There's a connecting door in there to the exhibition room. It's painted shut and has a display case hard up to it on the other side but if you press right up close against the thin wooden panelling you can hear perfectly well what's happening in the room next door.

We both listen as Richard finishes taking the ladies' entrance money and then announces that so far as any merchandising is concerned he's on commission and that he has a consumptive wife and three starving ragamuffin children to support. The ladies laugh, they know he's only joking. He sells them all guides and pencils and postcards and bookmarks and there seems to be some sort of competition going on between them to see who can spend the most money and please Richard the most. As he chats away Richard asks, remembers, then uses all their names. He explains that the contents of the display cases in the exhibition room are just a tiny selection of the contents of the drawers and cupboards of the house next door.

'What's that round your neck, Margaret? Is it what I think it is? That's a watch fob, isn't it, where have you had that from? I bet you nicked it, didn't you?'

'Oh. No,' she says, and even through half an inch of multiply painted pine you can feel her blushing.

'Shall I go in, Bruce?' Linda whispers. 'Shall I go in and stop him? I think I should stop him.'

'Can I look?' he says and Margaret must've unhooked it because next minute Richard says, 'Yeah, that's Birmingham; see the anchor and then that letter inside a lozenge, that's Birmingham about 1850. Now if you look over here there's one in this case. It belonged to Walter's dad but yours is much nicer. Do you still have the chain?'

'No,' she says, 'when Grandad died he left the watch and chain to my sister and she sold it, but my grandma always wore this around her neck. He gave it to her when they were courting and she left it to me.'

'Well,' he says, 'I think that's brilliant. It's a really lovely thing and you're keeping your past alive by wearing it and that's kind of the whole point of this house. When you walk round next door I'm sure you'll all recognise stuff your parents and your grandparents had and that's fine, nostalgia is fine, but what's really interesting about the house, apart from the lives of William and Walter and how they responded to the death of their parents, is that this place helps to explain how things are now, and when you've been round today, and when you get home and use a microwave or an electric kettle and switch the telly on or talk on the phone it'll feel different and it will be different and that'll be because you've been to the Hays House.

'Anyway, sorry to get all conceptual on you, ladies – can you tell I used to work in an art college? So shall we watch the tape or what?'

We hear the curtains in the bay swishing shut and the ladies fidgeting and shuffling their feet in the darkness, waiting for the film to begin.

The tape starts with tinkly *Listen with Mother*-style piano music and then some no-hope actor, doing his very best *Antiques Roadshow* voice, begins to speak . . .

No. 9 Maple Grove, Gateford was the home of the Hay family from 1905. It is a typical example of a well-to-do tradesman's house in a provincial town at the beginning of the last century and, because the family who lived there were so opposed to change, it has remained unaltered since the early 1930s. Down to the 1931 calendar on the wall of the dining room, there is barely a trace of the last seventy years.

In 1931 William Hay, a grocer and seeds merchant and father of two sons, William and Walter, died suddenly whilst shutting up shop one evening. This was such a devastating blow to the family that they changed nothing in the house from that day hence.

Father's pipes and tobacco pouch still stand on the side-table in the dining room, his hats and coats still hang on the pegs in the hall.

Nine years later Florence Hay, the boys' mother, also died and from this time on, her two sons lived on the surface of the house, existing entirely in the past. Walter, the younger son, took over the family business and William returned from London to look after the house. The brothers had no telephone, radio, television or central heating, and visitors to the house today step back over three-quarters of a century.

William died in 1991 aged ninety-six. He was the last of the Hay family. He bequeathed the entire contents of 9 Maple Grove, another property in Gateford, and the majority of his estate to the English Trust.

The English Trust was eventually able to buy the freehold of both Nos. 7 and 9 Maple Grove, and has made every effort to preserve the house exactly as it was discovered.

The Hay Family

William Hay senior was born in 1864 in Kenton-in-Ashfield, Nottinghamshire. His family had been blacksmiths there for generations, but in 1886 he and his elder brother, George, moved to Gateford. George had borrowed £700 from his family to set himself up as a grocer with a shop in the marketplace. At first William was employed by George, but after only three years he bought his brother out and prospered so readily that, when the premises he was renting came up for sale in 1903, he was able to buy them outright, together with an inn with several cottages.

At that time Gateford was a good trading town. It was situated in an expanding mining area and also for nearly two centuries had become firmly established as the market town serving the Dukeries, the name given locally to the large country estates in the area. Opposite William's shop, on the other side of the square, was David Wall, a butcher and local councillor whose business was equally prosperous.

Mr Wall fathered seven children and it was to his third child, Rose, that William Hay was married on 19 September 1894.

William Hay continued to thrive and, by 1905, he was sufficiently comfortable to contemplate moving from his rooms over the shop in the marketplace to a semi-detached house in Maple Grove, a respectable middle-class street on the outskirts of town. He and Rose had three sons: William, born in 1895, Walter in 1896, and David, who passed on in infancy in 1902. William and Walter were well educated, both attending King Egbert's Grammar School in Gateford.

Their education was curtailed by the First World War, when both boys were conscripted into the army. William joined the 4th Leicestershire Regiment, much to his disgust. He called it a 'mining regiment', and would have preferred to join the more fashionable and dapperly outfitted Sherwood Foresters. Walter was demobbed in 1919 and joined his father in the family business, while William went to King's College London to read English, which he later taught at the City of London College.

William's lodgings in London cost him £6 a month. The story goes that from his £30 monthly salary as a teacher he put the bulk of the remainder into Marks & Spencer shares. Through thrifty living and shrewd investment these shares alone were worth over £150,000 by the time of his death. When in August 1937 William resigned his teaching post, after a disagreement over his salary, he continued to spend most weeks in London until his mother's death in 1940. He passed his days a man of leisure: his diaries record visits to the National Gallery and the British Museum reading room. Every Friday he caught the 1.45 p.m. train home to Gateford.

After their parents' demise, William and Walter established a routine which did not falter for the next forty years. Every day Walter cycled to the shop in the marketplace, while William stayed at home cleaning, cooking and tending the garden. William played the dominant role in this relationship; he would not allow a telephone, radio or television. Walter finally bought a car in the 1960s, but he was forced to keep it at the shop and use his bicycle to get home. Every evening, after closing the shop, he would call in at his cousin's home across the street to listen to the 6 o'clock news on the radio.

Every Sunday the brothers went to St Augustine's Church and sat in the same pew. After lunch they would walk up to the marketplace, in their matching black bowler hats and blue serge suits, to inspect the shop and their other property in Gateford. In later years they were known to local people as the tin-tin men. Both were avid gardeners and Walter nurtured a large collection of cacti in his greenhouse in the back garden; both were also fascinated by local history.

The House

No. 9 Maple Grove was built in 1900. From the outside it is typical of many hundreds of thousands of such houses built around the turn of the nineteenth century. It has retained its sash-windows painted in traditional style to imitate wood-graining, and has an open porch leading to a grained front door with acid-etched glass. The railings were removed during the Second World War, much to William's annoyance. In October 1941 he wrote to Gateford Borough Council explaining that 'such railings are necessary to exclude cattle, dogs, etc from the gardens'. His protest was ignored, but the railings were not taken away until March 1943, when William received compensation of 7s 6d. Typically, William had made detailed measurements before their removal, and working from his original drawings the English Trust has reinstated both railings and gates.

'What's up, Margaret? You looked like you wanted to say something just then.'

'Richard's really not meant to do that, Bruce,' Linda hisses, her ear to the connecting door. 'He's not supposed to stop the tape, nobody's ever done that before. If anybody wants to ask questions they should wait until the end.'

'Oh it's nothing really,' Margaret says, 'but I remember that. I remember when they took all the railings, they even took the gates from the churchyard. And I remember they sandbagged the town hall and the library and the bank and my mother gave them her best saucepans to turn into Spitfires.'

'And do you know what happened to those gates and railings, ladies? The ones which were supposed to be melted down and turned into tin hats, rifles, bullets or whatever, do you know what actually happened to them?'

'No,' Margaret says.

'Well, at the end of the war they were all dumped in the sea.'

'Is that right, Bruce?' Linda whispers. 'Is that what happened to all those lovely ornamental gates and railings?'

'Yes, dear, I'm afraid it is, I read it somewhere. He's right, he does seem to know his stuff, this one.'

'Anyway, for what it's worth, shall I tell you what I'd have done?' Richard says. 'I'd have melted them all down and turned them into gates and railings, and if you think that's silly just ask yourself how sensible it was to chuck the whole lot in the bloomin' sea. Anyway, back to the tape.'

The exterior of the house has been left unscathed by the DIY boom of the last forty years, but the true uniqueness of the building only becomes clear when the visitor enters the house. The hall and dining room are papered in the dark colours popular at the time, all the original doors, skirtings, fireplaces and cornices are still in place, and there is a density of furnishing typical of the Edwardian age.

William Hay senior bought 9 Maple Grove for £766 1s 6d in 1905, and proceeded to have it decorated from top to bottom before moving in with his family. All the rooms were papered, with fashionable patterned borders, a lavatory was plumbed into the bathroom, a gas stove fitted to augment the original kitchen range, and new sockets and pendants were added to the rudimentary electrical system already installed in the house.

We now come to the tour of the house. Visitor guides will be on hand to answer any questions which you, the visitor, may have, but the basic facts are outlined here.

The Dining Room

In 1940 William drew up an inventory of the ground floor of the house which included details of every last tin and packet of food in the kitchen cupboards. In this inventory William refers to the front room as the dining room and lists the contents of the room under that heading. However, as this room faces south, the Hay family also used it as their everyday living room. It was one of only two rooms in the house where a fire was regularly lit, but the brothers, being careful with their money, economised on coal by placing bricks in the grate.

This room is characteristically cluttered and contains some of the family's best furniture, much of it bought by William's father at country-house sales. The dining table and chairs were a wedding present to the Hays. Against the right-hand wall is an impressive walnut cabinet, while in the corner to the left of the window is a good example of a Gateford-made Windsor chair.

There are touching reminders of William Hay senior in this room too. On the right of the fireplace is a calendar with a picture of two puppies, and on a side-table to the left, his pipes and tobacco pouch.

The Sitting Room

This room was Rose Hay's sanctuary: her Bible sits on the table, her embroidery basket on the piano stool. There are china and glass ornaments on all the surfaces, and a French Empire-style clock on the mantelpiece, while the 1920s Sanderson curtains and matching chair covers add a sense of refined femininity to the room.

From here the visitor should go up the stairs to the first floor and double back towards the front of the house.

Walter's Bedroom

Walter returned home to help his father with the grocery business after being demobbed in 1919 and it is likely this is the reason why he took over the larger bedroom previously occupied by his elder brother William, who was still living in London at the time.

On the wall behind the bed are two embroidered frames, worked by Rose Hay in 1881, containing photographs of her parents. When Walter retired from the grocery business in the early 1960s, some of the tools of the family trade found their way back to the house and on the small table to the right of the window are a selection of bamboo seed and tea measures.

The Parents' Bedroom

This room remains exactly as it looked on Rose's death in 1940 and is amongst the most poignant and best-preserved parts of the house. On the oak dressing-table are photographs of William (left) and Walter (right) as infants, and a leather box for their father's detachable collars. The bed has been covered with newspaper to keep the dust off the covers and various articles of Rose and William Senior's clothing have been laid between the blankets as a way of storing them flat.

From here we go up the stairs to the second-floor front bedroom.

William's Bedroom

This is the smallest bedroom. It was used by William until the day he went into hospital in 1986, leaving the better bedrooms on the first floor untouched as a memorial to his family. It was in this room that he kept his most prized possessions – his books. These books – mostly local history and English literature – are shielded from the light by a cloth hung over the glass-fronted bookcase.

The little rocking chair under the window was a gift from his mother on his fifth birthday.

The Store Cupboard

Curiously, this linen cupboard on the second-floor landing was used by the Hay brothers as a provision store. Some of the tins in here date back to the early 1930s.

Richard stops the tape again.

'Just out of interest, how many of you lot keep their tins in an upstairs wardrobe? No, I thought not. I don't know what you think, ladies, but it strikes me these two guys were crazy in the coconut.'

The Lumber Room

Originally a maid's room, this became the store-room of the Hays household. The floor is covered with old newspapers and it was here that the English Trust discovered objects, carefully packed in labelled boxes, as diverse as an unworn pair of patent boots, an ARP warden's steel helmet, old tins and many years of bottled jam made by the Hays from fruit grown on their allotment garden opposite the house on the other side of Maple Grove. William's spade, still in pristine condition, leans against the wall.

Retrace your steps to the first floor and walk towards the back of the house.

The Back Bedroom

This room served as a second storeroom. There is an engraving of Kenton Hall dated 1897. A square of paper pasted to the back of the frame describes – in William's handwriting – its past history in great detail.

The Bathroom

This very bare and functional room would have been considered a great luxury at the time it was installed. The room is unheated and the bare walls are decorated with oil paint for ease of cleaning.

Return downstairs and, passing the coats and

hats, some of them belonging to William Hay senior, go into the kitchen.

The Kitchen

The kitchen is bare and in complete contrast to the cosy image of period kitchens so often conjured by popular memory. William baked bread every Saturday night in this kitchen, using his mother's recipe and kitchen utensils.

Leave the house by the kitchen door and, after looking round the garden, return to the car park down the side passage.

Finally, please remember that, although small, this is nevertheless a historic building. Take care not to touch the walls and please treat the property with the respect it deserves.

'And no spitting,' says Richard.

Y ou know what I'd like to do now? You know
what I really feel like doing? Wind my fist into a
thick knot of frizzy perm, drag Kay up to the top
landing, smash her on the head with something blunt
and Victorian, chuck her denim skirt up over her back,
pull her pink polyester top down off her shoulders so
it cheers the cow's tits up, points them up in hello-
pleased-to-see-you-style, ease away the gusset of her
£1.99 Poundstretcher pants and expose the target
area. Sweaty nylon briefs. Nylon, sweaty and brief
maybe with just the tiniest hint of a skidmark, no
lumps, thank you, just a hint of shit. Oh ho, what shall
we go for today, I wonder: the pink or the brown? Fold
her over the blanket chest . . .

Back door rattles and Kay comes in.

'Always twist that knob the wrong way,' she says.
'Every single morning. Never been very good with
knobs. Who's this?'

And Richard's on his feet.

'I'm Richard,' he says. 'The new long-term volunteer.
Nice to meet you, you must be Kay, the housekeeper.
Bruce's told me all about you.'

'Has he now?' she says, her face stiffening. 'You

don't want to take no notice of Bruce, he's a wanker. That's right, isn't it, Bruce?'

'Yes, Kay, that's right.'

'Tell Richard what you are, Bruce.'

'I'm a wanker.'

'What else are you, Bruce?'

'I'm a dirty man who doesn't deserve to live here.'

'Hear that, Richard?'

'Yeah, er yes, Kay.'

'While ago now Bruce asked me into the office, said he had something to show me. Unzipped his cords and showed me a very small thing. Begged me to suck his dick. That's right, isn't it, soldier?'

'Yes, Kay.'

'I never told Linda but if need be I will. Then I'll tell my Gary. He's strong, is my Gary, comes from lifting lumps of concrete all day, and if my Gary ever found out, well . . . Any bother from this one, just let me know. Right, Bruce, I'll be back in ten minutes. I'll have a coffee. Two sugars, not too milky.'

'Yes, Kay.'

Kay goes up the stairs in our house. I hear her unbolt the connecting door at the top of the attic stairs which leads to her cleaning cupboard and then into the Hays next door. I sit at the kitchen table, clench my face, my arse, and hope Richard can't see I'm shaking.

Richard clears his throat.

'Is that right, Bruce – did you really do that?'

'No, Richard, it was a misunderstanding.'

'How long ago?'

'About a year.'

I go upstairs for a wash. When it gets like this I have a wash. I go into the guest bedroom, lock myself in the en suite bathroom, strip off and I have a wash. It's clean in there and it's different. It doesn't feel like our house.

I like to imagine I'm a different person in a different town. I'm here on business, important business, and I've got half an hour before I have to appear at a pukka do and make a speech. I'll start with a joke, maybe the one about the talking frog, and then get to the serious bit. I'll make them laugh then I'll really impress them.

I fill the basin and siphon a big dollop of liquid soap into my left hand. I do my neck, my shoulders and my armpits then I stand on the towel and put a foot in the sink. I wash the four spaces between the five toes and then do the other foot. After that, I squidge some more soap into my right hand and do my cock.

My limp redundant cock. Always in that order. Order of importance. Feet useful, cock not. Feet then cock. Feet and inches. Two soapy hands working the magic, one on the nuts, the other fingering around the shaft. Nothing, not a flicker.

I soap my arse and hang it over the edge of the basin for a rinse. I towel myself dry and get dressed all except for the shirt. I run a fresh basin, wash my face, dry my face, slick back my hair. I button my shirt, smooth the cravat back around my throat and stare at myself in the mirror. A bit grey and baggy perhaps, but I reckon I could still cut it with the ladies. Nothing happening in the trousers, nothing much upstairs. Not too bad for fifty.

I don't know what lasses think. And I used to love that. Not knowing what they thought. It's all right when you're young, it seems like it's worth the effort. I don't know what happens to them as they get older and you get older.

You meet, you dance. You fuck. You fall in love. You fuck some more, you marry. You dance at your wedding, afterwards you make love formally. You get to know each other, to respect each other as human beings, and it stops happening. It goes from coming naturally, the lasses go from coming naturally, to you having to try so hard, to them knowing you have to try so hard, to them not wanting you to try so hard, to you having to try so hard to get hard and even if you do, you have to try so hard to pretend that you've not had to try so hard to get hard, that after you've got hard you're trying so hard to get them interested that after a while it's just easier to slide off to the bogs for a wank.

No matter how hard you try it doesn't happen. You don't dance, you don't get hard, you don't fuck and you argue. Sometimes I feel like telling Gary myself, explain to him that all I am is a dirty joke, and shake hands. Tell him that I've not done it in three years – let alone had a proper hard-on – and that, when I did get one that afternoon a year ago, as I pressed up against the photocopier and felt a stiff one brewing, I felt like having it stuffed and mounted.

It would have been wrong to waste it, a sin, a crime.

I'm sure he'd be fine about it. Christ, all the sex he gets. Whenever I see Kay and Gary together they're at it. Undressing each other with their eyes and later with their fingers. Matching trainers, matching joggies, matching tops, matching orgasms. We had a Friends of the Hays House garden fête last summer and I'm certain Gary fingered Kay's bush in the bushes. All I required was one little shufti and that would have tided me over for the next three years. I think the Trust would have approved of that, just so long as it wasn't visible from the road. She's lovely is Kay, she's lovely. She's bubbly, she's busty and she's a laugh. Sometimes she tells me I look smart.

Secretly I thought she'd always fancied me, then I realised all it was was that secretly I'd always fancied her and anyway, when I came out of the office that afternoon with a king dong hard-on and a prayer on my lips for either pair of her lips, I thought it'd be OK. If I had the chance to explain, me and Gary'd shake hands, maybe even have a drink and a laugh about it. Then he'd kill me.

I like Gary. He makes me laugh. He's a big burly chap, an ex-para and it shows. He irons his jeans, wears white trainers which he cleans with a tooth-brush and he won't let Kay do the washing up – not up to his standards, he says. He stands up straight, he sits up straight and he's straight down the line, is Gary, but he walks with a limp. He landed badly and broke his leg, says he saw it happening in slow motion, the ground rushing up at him, his leg bending back all wrong and him thinking shit that shouldn't be happening. He only felt the real pain next day and every single day for the next five years. Gary reckons his leg predicts the weather, damp weather anyway.

Gary flew to Spain for his honeymoon. Halfway across his stomach tightened, he had an unbearable urge to stand. Felt he should be doing something. Then he realised. Gary sat back down, got himself a whisky, slipped his arm round Kay and started to laugh. He didn't have to jump out this time.

Gary makes dwarfs for a living – that's what he calls 'em anyway. They make all sorts at Kenton Precast. Precast balustrade, precast patio blocks, precast bird baths, precast sundials, precast statues, all kinds of horrible precast shit, but Gary specialises in the gnomes.

If I've told him once I've told him a hundred times. They're gnomes, Gary, as in the gnomes of Dulwich, dwarfs are different, they're . . . well, they're just different.

Gary mixes up a batch of concrete then tips it out into a row of latex moulds. He's told me this in great detail, several times. The rubber moulds are set up in sandboxes and Gary moves down the line kicking the sides of the boxes with his Toetectors to get rid of bubbles then leaves the concrete to set.

Gary loves his Toetectors. He's obsessed. Give him half a chance and he'll talk about them for hours. Linda's got one of Gary's dwarfs – she won in last year's Friends of the Hays House Christmas raffle. It's a freak, a second, that's how come Kenton Precast let Gary bring it home. Gary can't have kicked this one's box hard enough. There must've been an airlock over its face and there's just a big empty scoop where its mouth ought to be.

It lives in the front garden, lurking in the bushes just inside the gate. You can see it from our sitting room but definitely not from the road – the Trust wouldn't allow that. Linda loves it, she calls it Stony, she even says hello to the damn thing on her way out of the house sometimes.

Stupid tart – does she really think it's going to talk back? How the hell's it going to do that without a mouth.

I hate the fucking thing but Bruno quite likes it. Every morning and every night he waits while I un-latch the gate to the drive and then just as it's time to get moving he cocks his leg and pisses right in Stony's ugly little face.

When I come downstairs I feel clean and useful. Demented but clean and useful, as Linda always likes to say. Richard makes me a coffee, empties the ash-tray, tells me that Kay's gone, and changes the subject.

'You got kids, Bruce?'

'Yes, one. His name's Richard too, actually. He married a German girl, name of Ingrid.'

'And?'

'And nothing. We don't talk any more.'

'Ooh err,' he says, 'that's a rubbish song.'

Actually I quite like Cliff, especially at Christmas, but I let it go and I explain to Richard about Richard and about how last Christmas I made a joke while that song was playing, substituting the word talk with shag about his wife and how they'd been married two years and still no sign of kids. I shouldn't have, I know, but it was only a joke.

Richard's back in the exhibition room, Linda's in the office and I've got nothing to do. Two more timed visits and we're done for the day. I smoke three more fags on the trot.

It doesn't need it but I mop the kitchen floor just like I did yesterday when it didn't need it either. The doorbell rings. Linda shouts me to get it and it rings again.

I park the mop and get the door.

'Oh hello, Bruce, and how are you this afternoon?'

It's Simon. Jumped-up, over-educated twat. Regional Director of the Trust and still in his twenties. He prides himself on his hands-on approach, does Simon. Likes to turn up unannounced, informal and relaxed, take the band off his ponytail, stroke his silly bumfluff beard and put the shits up everybody.

I show him through to the kitchen, drop the ashtray into the bin and open the back door to drain off some of the smoke.

'Has somebody been smoking in here, Bruce?'

'Er no, Simon, yes. Must be the new volunteer. I'll put him straight.'

'Yes, you do that, make sure you do that. Now be a good chap and tell Linda I'm here.'

I turn to go and bump straight into Linda.

'Hello, Simon,' she says. 'This is an unexpected pleasure.'

She does it every time. Every time Simon turns up Linda's voice goes up. It goes up an octave and she starts talking like the Queen. She knows she does it and she knows I know. It always makes me laugh.

Let's get one thing straight, Lindypoos – I'm the posh one round here. Around these parts I'm the chap with the nobby top-notch diction. I say, Linda, my good woman, if your perspicuity was at a premium you'd have noticed that by now. I really must insist. Make mine a Pimm's and put a fucking horse in it. Super, eh? Spiffing.

I'm the local lad who sounded like wet bread, but lost the accent doublequicktime and talked posh to fit in with all the posh little boys at big posh school, left school and joined the army, talked posh and didn't fit in, left the army still talking posh and don't fit in anywhere any more.

Linda spots the grin straight off and orders me out, gives me my marching orders. Says Bruno requires a walk even though he doesn't. My little canine chum's slumbering, pushing out the zeds and chasing wabbits all over doggy dreamworld – you can see him twitching. The poor little sod's fast asleep in his basket. I fetch the lead from the back of the kitchen door, latch it to his collar and he wakes.

Bruno hauls himself upright, has a good shake and we're off.

I still think Yorkshire. If I meet someone in the road I still think 'All right then, youth' if it's a bloke, 'lass' if it's a lady. Which is what we say round here and it's a polite affection, but it comes out 'Hello, how are you this fine afternoon?' which is affectation.

And I know they're thinking who the hell does that stuck-up chuff think he is? A lad from the Mountford Estate talking posh like that. He did a picture of an avocet once, wrote about a boat and had the stupidest name in town – I've heard if he sees a woman's twat he legs it. So what's he got to feel so smug about?

I should be angry at Simon, talking to me like that. Born with full silver dinner service wedged up his arse, that one. He really is posh, the genuine article, and he knows full well I'm not.

He treats me like dirt. I should feel angry about that, but I don't. These days I feel hardly anything but tired.

Bruno pauses just inside the front gate, cocks his leg and gives Stony a good squirt. Whahey, nice shootin', Tex – that really was a good one.

I bend down to take a closer look at the little misshapen concrete fella and notice his face has gone bright-green. You wouldn't think dog piss could do that to a reject dwarf's face but it does.

I spend a lot of time in the gunshop. You have to ring the bell, Frank puts down his *Shooting Times* and lays his panatella in the ashtray. He flicks a switch on the counter, the frame buzzes and you're in. All I want is a cheap one. Spanish AYA Yeoman. Side by side, single trigger, fixed choke, non-ejector, no poncy engraving. A proper farmer's gun. I'd have the stock steamed and fitted, bull up the barrels a bit and get maybe a better case, but a cheap one'd do me just fine.

Frank's Fieldsports & Country Pursuits. It smells of oil in there. Waxed clothes, wellies, walking sticks and cordite. I'm a non-starter for a shotgun certificate. Frank knows about the medication.

'Of all people, Bruce,' he always says, 'you're the man. Worked hard all your life, worked with guns all your life, you've the attitude, the dog, the clothes – Christ, Bruce, you've even got the haircut.'

I flick through Frank's *Shooting Times*. 'Town Gun' by Colin Woodhouse, a little column tucked away in the back pages amongst the various ads for rough shooting and even rougher 0898 girls. Colin runs an MOT testing station weekdays and he sometimes drops in little anecdotes about a Moggy Thou he's worked on or a baby Austin he's tested for emissions. Weekends he's Town Gun.

He's at one with nature is our Colin. At one with it till it gets the wrong side of two quarter-choked barrels and an eighth of an ounce of barely subsonic lead at any rate. He loves to be outside does Colin, he slips a friendly farmer twenty quid, MOTs his car for free and wanders the soft green landscape blasting the shit out of anything with a face.

Town Gun shoots on the weekends. He drives a vintage Landy, bags the odd woody and he always gets rained on. Sometimes he gets lucky and blows up a bunny.

He's got an Aga. We've got an Aga.

What I really want is a gun. I need a gun nearly as badly as I need a fuck. I can't even take this seriously any more, and this is what I really want. If I could just get hold of a gun and a box of cartridges I could be happy.

Linda's not a happy bunny when I get home. Head in her hands at the kitchen table and paper everywhere. She turns her face up towards me then drops it again. I feel guilty, like I've done something, but I've been out so there's no way it can be me this time.

'Hello, Lindy, what's up?'

'Simon wants me to run a Victorian Christmas Fayre at Clumber. He suggested it might be a good idea anyway and coming from Simon you know what that means, Bruce. It means we have to do it. It's an order.'

Her face looks red and puffy. She's been crying and as she goes through what needs doing – the putting the house to bed, then the invites, the cake-making, the demonstrations, the decorations for the Fayre and after that all the preparations for the Friends' Christmas Meal – she starts to cry again.

Doorbell rings eight-thirty sharp. Linda gets the door, lets Richard into the hallway, he bounds into the kitchen and makes us all a coffee.

'So what's the sport plan for today?' he asks.

Linda fires him a blank look. 'Check the diary,' she snaps, 'the black one in the office. You've been here a month for God's sake, Richard, you should know what to do by now.'

'OK,' he says, his face in his boots, and shuffles out.

'By the phone,' she shouts after him. 'Have you taken your pills, Bruce?'

'Yes, dear, just started on the new ones this morning.'

Two minutes later he's back.

'So you know what you're doing now, Richard,' I bark at him.

'Yes, Bruce.'

'Good man, good man. So what did it say in the diary?' And I'm thinking this is great, somebody to order around.

'Shut up, Bruce,' Linda hisses. 'What does it say, Richard?'

'It says strip all the tat out of next door, box it up

65

and take it to the nearest junk shop, go to B and Q, buy white paint and apply it top to bottom, smarten the old place up, get some students in, take the rent and retire to the Bahamas. Looks like we're in for a busy day.'

Richard necks his coffee and goes back in the office. Me and Linda hear the clang of the filing cabinet then the chink of money.

'What's he doing?' I ask without looking at her.

'Cashing up, Bruce. There's only one visit today and that's prepaid, so we might as well bank what we've got and just leave a float for the souvenirs – if there's any left – if Richard didn't sell them all last week, that is,' and I can hear in her voice that she's smiling.

'He's all right, isn't he? One thing, Bruce.'

'Linda?'

'Don't boss him around. You know what happens and we've had this conversation before. This house is my responsibility, not yours. There's been complaints and we've lost people before, good people, because of it.'

Linda shouts Richard in from the office.

'Sorry I snapped, Richard. You OK?'

'Ye-ahs,' he says in a fake Mexican accent. 'It ees not a *problema*.'

'Will you take the money to NatWest for me, please, when you've totted up?'

'Sure thing, Lindy baby,' he grins, and curls his lip like Elvis.

Richard stands, fills the electric kettle and flicks it on.

'You fuck offee, Bruce?' he asks and Linda laughs.

I turn and look in his eyes and we're leaned up against the same kitchen unit. I get this feeling. It must be the pills. I have a real feeling of time and where we are in it. Butterscotch kitchen unit from MFI, green onyx work-top also from Made For Idiots and the three of us. Him and me and my wife. And then I figure this little cunt's six inches taller than me. Wiry, and he looks pretty fit. But I could have him. I reckon I could have him. If it came to it I could deck that little fucker. He can say what the fuck he likes to my wife and so long as he does it with a smile it'll be OK. She can yell at him and he'll comply. He'll bide his time and take the piss then she'll apologise. He'll charm the pants off her then she'll beg him to let Lindy suck his dick. But it's not that. There's something, something about Richard, something that you can't help but like. He is genuinely happy to be here and it shows. He's interested and he wants to learn.

Humble and cocky is a tricky one, a hard one to pull off. But he's got it all right, and I realise I'm not having this one, not without a fight at any rate. To be honest if at this precise moment I walked in from walking Bruno and found Richard fucking Linda on the kitchen table I wouldn't be the least surprised. If I walked in from walking Linda and found him fucking Bruno on the kitchen table I wouldn't be that surprised either except it's definitely not hygienic. Whatever it is he's got it.

Linda wants to suck his dick and have him call her

baby. The whole world wants to suck his dick and do that and knowing Richard he'd humbly let 'em then make a joke about it after.

When you look at him close he's an ugly little fucker, but he acts handsome and it works every time. It does and I should know. He reminds me of me at that age except whatever he's got he really has got and I never really had it. I thought I did but I didn't. I just pretended, and even that worked for a while. Christ, you should have seen me. Bulled up, lumped up, pumped up, pissed up and ready to perform.

Somebody tapping at the back door.

Regimental Christmas Bash, Retford Civic Centre 1973. My sergeant-major hunched over the railing outside, the vomit screaming from his mouth, his nose and, I swear, his ears.

Councillor Ralph Hardwick takes to the stage. He presides over the proceedings, presents a charity cheque and introduces the band. A volunteer orchestra who strictly should not have volunteered. Pubs all shut and each of us with a book of raffle tickets, every one a winner, each one a guaranteed pint.

I saw, I conquered, and later – just out of sight of the fire exit – Linda came.

First woman in my life who actually took a shine to me. First woman in my life I hadn't paid for.

God knows, I'm paying for it now.

'Bruce, will you get the door.'

There's a cold white spot in Retford. A cold spot. Just out of sight of the fire exit – which, incidentally, in contravention of the fire regulations, is almost completely blocked by crated empties – a draughty corner where I exited before I fired. In a jenell just off Councillor Ralph Hardwick Drive, which is why he was there, and somewhere down that alley, there's a stain probably invisible now to the human eye but detectable to DNA testers if they knew what they were looking for.

And one day there'll be a navy-blue plaque.

ON THIS SPOT BRUCE GLASSCOCK

PROPERLY

AND

FOR FREE

AND

FOR THE FIRST TIME

CAME

ON HIS FUTURE WIFE

AND

WAS

LATER

INDUSTRIALLY

SICK.

PLEASE DO NOT THROW STONES AT THIS NOTICE.

'BRUCE, WILL YOU GET THE DOOR.'

I hope it's Rebecca from next door. I like Rebecca.

She's clever, she's sweet and her ex-husband – who travels in baby food – must be clinically insane. He fucked up big time.

He left her for Julie.

Julie Goodwright, the former Miss Kenton Park. A bonny, big-breasted, long-limbed, small-brained lass with her own salon and tanning cabin, a vague idea that she was royalty, a grotesque sideline in nail art and a very irritating habit of ducking her head and flicking all her hair back while she was talking at you. Julie's red Renault Clio was unfortunately involved in a head-on collision with Duggie the Dinosaur – a cut-off old-time single-decker bus with a winch on the back who goes out in all weathers recovering his mates – and Julie was rendered mentally defective by the impact.

Julie lost her marbles but kept her looks. Hair flicker to window licker in about nine seconds.

Julie took to wandering the streets in a yellow bikini and jumping out of the bushes on the central reservation of the A57 and flashing her manicured bush at passing motorists. Julie took to going pike fishing with Mark Kyte the local nutter, stripping off and running naked around the banks of Ulley reservoir, which puts the fear of God into the local anglers but apparently does not scare the pike.

I like Rebecca. I like her a lot. She's always smiling, she's a friend and a Friend. We have Friends at the Hays, people who give money and spend time helping out. People who care about the place.

There never was before. Linda did that, got a group of people together, made a club of it, made them feel special and made it pay. The Trust are sniffy about houses like ours, like Linda's.

Simon Says. Oh yeah, Simon says all right. Hold up both your hands – on the one we have the polite, on the other we have the vernacular.

Polite is big places, crumbling stately piles with a Queen Anne front and a Mary Ann behind, a much better class of bluebottle buzzing round their industrial-sized bins, extensive grounds, an army of staff, a family mausoleum and a tearoom.

Vernacular is the Hays and more recently McCartney's house. The toffs at head office hate it but we're, Linda, is creaming them at present.

'Bruce, will you . . .'

'Steady on, gel,' says Richard. 'I'll get it, your old fella's away with the fairies.'

It is Rebecca.

'I got your message,' she smiles, 'and I came straight round.'

Linda introduces her to Richard.

'Hell-ow,' he purrs. At least the little cunt's got taste.

Rebecca. Blue jeans, pink T-shirt, white trainers, no socks and – I can hardly bring myself to look – no bra.

Rebecca. Soft, lovely, kind, generous, gentle, warm-hearted Rebecca. Beautiful hair, beautiful eyes, long shapely legs, super complexion and an . . .

'And how are you this morning, Bruce?'

'Outstanding pair of tits.'

I don't know who said it.
Who said never go back.
Never apologise.
But they had the right idea.
I went back.
I apologised.
I thought I'd just thought it.
And so I thought if I told Rebecca that I thought I'd
only thought it.
If I told her I only meant to think it.
That I thought all I'd done was to think it.
It didn't work.
I go upstairs for a wash.
Keep it clean.
Feet and inches.
The one about the petshop.
With
a
wasp
in
the
window.

By the time I'm back downstairs Rebecca's gone. Richard and Linda are in the office chattering about something. I press my head against the door.

'Blimey,' Richard says, 'talk about speaking your mind – not very PC but very funny all the same.'

'What's PC, Richard?'

'Many things, Linda. Personal computer, pocket calculator, purple corset, people carrier, pink clouds, pale custard, proper charlie, pure cheek, polite coversation, pigeon club, poorly cats, plastic-coated, pickled cabbage, potato crisp, porky crunch, primitive compass, personal crisis, promising career, past caring, probable cause, previous conviction, pencil case, public convenience, popular culture, pin cushion, porcelain cat, prize cucumber, primary colour, private courtyard, playing card, professional criminal, plaster cast, perfect couple, pristine condition, prime cut, pre-cut, pre-coloured, pre-chilled, pre-cooked, pre-copied, pre-counted, pre-combed, pre-covered, pre-coppered . . .'

'Richard!'

'Er, and obviously police constable. But in this particular case: politically correct.'

'What's that when it's at home?'

'Basically everything which Bruce is not.'

'I should have left him, I know I should. I should have left him years ago, but it's too late now. I should have left him. In the '70s like my mother told me. She's in my dreams sometimes and she's still telling me to leave him, but I daren't.'

'He'd not be able to cope. He'd probably kill himself.'

I hear Linda's chair scrape back, footsteps across the hollow floor, and I'm not nearly quick enough. She whips the door open and catches me lurking in the hallway.

'Car keys, Bruce.'

'Wh . . . ?'

'Car keys, Bruce.'

'But, but . . .'

'So Richard can get to the bank.'

'You're letting him drive?'

'You *can* drive, Richard?' Linda shouts into the office.

'Oh yeah,' he calls back, 'like a bar steward. Last driving job I had, I took all four-wheel arches and both mirrors off a Transit. Foreman of the company I worked for – British Plasterboard – said it wouldn't fit through the space between the canteen and the strip-metal store, but it did. Just not all in one go.'

'Will you take the money to NatWest for me, please?'

'Cool,' he says, 'like a backwards bank job, I move

like greased lightning through the mean streets of town, shake off the Old Bill, screech up to the bank, dive straight in there mob-handed and then, er, I hand over the dosh.'

'You can park in Bridge Place next door to the Cash and Carry, it's free parking if you're less than an hour. Go carefully for God's sake and don't forget to lock it.'

'Cool,' he says again. 'Two-lane blacktop, here we come, let's burn rubber.'

'Why do men turn into children when it comes to cars?'

'They just do, Linda,' Richard laughs. 'They just do. It's the law.'

'Garage key, Bruce.'

'No, it's OK, Linda, I'll get the car out.'

'You will not. Keys, Bruce. Now.'

Kitchen door rattles and Rebecca's back. We all file into the kitchen.

'Oh hi, Bruce. Linda, I've got the felt-tips you wanted and I've had a go at the drawing.'

'The what?'

'Well, it's actually not your business, Bruce, but Rebecca's very kindly offered to help me do the invites for the Christmas Fayre.'

'Why wasn't I told, why didn't you ask me to do the drawing? I used to be really good at drawing, used to love it when I was a kid. I drew a picture of an avocet once, it was so realistic you could have touched it and it would have flown away, in fact it was partly that which got me into –'

'Bruce, will you be quiet. If you want to help you can make us all a coffee – if you think you might be able to manage that. Do you fancy a quick one, Richard, before you go to the bank?'

'Oo err,' he says, 'there's always time for a quick one, but a coffee's fine.'

And Linda starts giggling and Rebecca joins in.

Two fully grown women giggling like schoolgirls, and Richard. They're all sat round the table smiling at each other, looking at Rebecca's drawing and telling her how good it is while I'm stood over by the worktop waiting while the kettle boils and feeling like a spare todger in a knocking establishment.

I pour three lots of boiling water into three mugs, spoon in three lots of amber powder, two brown sugars into the first one for Linda, and just for a second it strikes me that this would be the ideal time, the perfect moment to lean across and empty the rest of the kettle into Richard's crotch. Boil-in-the-bag bollocks. Uh ho yes. What a great idea. That'd keep the little fucker quiet for a while.

'You not having one, Bruce?' Richard asks.

'What?'

'You not fuck offee?'

'Er no, I thought I'd get the car out, warm her up for you. Distributor might be a bit damp.'

I love that little car. Red she is, grey upholstery and a double black stripe down each side. When I'm inside her I feel safe, I feel confident and I feel in control. She's got heated seats and a radio. Sometimes I talk to her. Tell her things about myself. Sometimes I just sing along.

I unhook the car keys from under the Historic Derbyshire calendar, fetch the garage key from the top of the cellar stairs and make for the back door. I'll be out of the house quicker that way but there's no chance and there never was.

'Bruce.'

I know the cow's about to shit on my strawberries. Any second now. I can feel it coming. She always does. Richard and Rebecca go quiet.

'Bruce.'

'Linda?'

'Bruce, where do you think you're going?'

'Linda, my sweet, I am perfectly capable of getting the fucking car out of the fucking garage.'

'How many times, Bruce, how many times have I told you. You do not use language like that in front of the volunteers.'

'But –'

'But nothing. Give me the bloody keys. Sorry, Rebecca, Richard, but this is what I have to put up with. There's enough to do without this, Bruce, now give me the keys.'

'No.'

'What?'

'No.'

'Look, I didn't want to have to do this. Have you read the notes that came with your tablets, the ones that say under no circumstances are you allowed to drive?'

I hand over the car keys.

I chucked those notes in the bin. The cow must have fished them out and read them.

'Which is the garage one, Bruce?'

Ah hah, I'm thinking, got you now, you fat bitch, and as I go to clench my hand round the proper key I realise it's a fist already.

'The little silver one. It says Egret on it.'

Linda hands Richard the keys.

'Get the car out, Richard, and bring it round the front. Ring the bell when you're ready and I'll bring the money out. Did you cope with the paying-in book?'

'Yeah.'

'Coins, notes, cheques, all that?'

'Yeah, all that.'

'Good. I'll countersign it in a minute, you get the car.'

Richard goes out the back door and I hear his footsteps down the side of the house. Give the little shit about ten minutes. I clip Bruno's lead to his collar and we step outside. This is going to be good.

What a beautiful morning. Bruno at my heel, my green hunter boots swishing through the dead leaves, my breath like smoke, the sun slanting low through the proud skeletons of the tall poplars skirting the back edge of the car park, a bright-blue sky, a nip in the air and everywhere the sights and scents of autumn.

Just the faintest whiff of death. That lovely, that precise, that sublime yet indefinable moment when mellow fruitfulness transcends overipe promise and slips inexorably into inevitable and silent decay. The rich cycle of the seasons – birth, growth, death, rebirth and all that old bollocks.

I sneeze and lemon snot splatters the back of my hand – just like you never see at the flicks. But I don't mind, not this morning at any rate, and as I wipe it away with a freshly laundered hand-stitched linen hanky it feels good just to be alive and good to be just the tiniest stitch in life's majestic tapestry.

I take a crisp double lungful of sweet autumn air then lean on the mossy five-bar gate to the car park and roll a fag.

Somebody really should take a photograph. 'Autumn Tints', they could call it. One man and his dog in perfect harmony, sweet comeuppance on its way and mother nature smiling down in all her faded glory. A perfect moment on a perfect morning at the perfect end of a perfectly shit year.

It'd probably sweep the board at the Gateford Photographic Society annual dinner dance and show.

But what's this? Something not quite right with this picture. Three figures milling round the front of the garage are completely shagging up the otherwise perfect composition of this idyllic autumnal scene and you can tell from their body language that something's up.

Linda's flushed red, Richard's waving his arms around and Rebecca, well, she's just looking radiant.

Linda snatches the keys off Richard and has a try.

'I can get it in but it won't turn. Are you sure this is the right key? Bruce, Bruce, could you come over here a minute, please?'

Think I must have gone a bit deaf. I'm sure I heard a voice just then, or maybe it was just a door squeaking or an animal being sick somewhere, and even if it was a voice I've not the faintest what it said – something about requiring my assistance, I believe – but that can't be right, now can it?

Of all the cigarettes I've got through in my time I reckon this must be the best-tasting one ever. Me? I think I'll just stay here if it's all the same to you, folks. Me and Bruno and the autumn tints, my lovely green wellies, my fragrant cigarette and the sunny sunshine.

'He can't have heard. Would you go and fetch him, Richard?'

'Do I have to?'

'Yes, if you wouldn't mind.'

'I do mind a bit, actually.'

'Just go and get him, please.'

'Zipperdidoodah zipperdi . . . Ah, Richard, what seems to be the trouble?'

'Can't get the key to work, Bruce,' he mumbles, staring at his shoes.

'Well, it's quite simple, my fine young fellow. You put it in the lock and you give it a turn. Didn't they teach you that at university, or maybe you've just got weak wrists. Shove it in and give a twist, man. Couldn't be easier.'

Off he goes. Back to the garage to have another go and this time he looks like he means business. I see him grab the keys off Linda and shove the tiny key marked Egret in the big lock marked Squire, and this time he uses both hands to try to get it to turn.

But it's no use.

'Bruce, would you come over here, please?'

I definitely heard something that time.

'Come on, old lad,' I say.

Bruno trots along after me and we move as one through the autumn tints till we reach the rusted corrugated-tin erection which constitutes the Hays House motor home and toolstore.

'Bruce, are you sure this is the right key?'

'Positive, my dear.'

'This is definitely the right key?'

'Absolutely so, Lindypops.'

'Well, it doesn't work. It won't turn.'

'Give it here, you silly woman. Let me try.' And I stand with my back to them, open my hand and pop the right key into the lock.

'There we go, just half a turn. Simple as that.'

I hand her back the keys.

'Not as useless as you like to make out, am I, my darling?'

'Er, no, Bruce. Thankyou.'

Well, well, well. Linda thanking me and in front of Richard and Rebecca too. Someone really should take a photograph.

M e? I feel so chipper now I can scarcely believe it's not butter and the old brainbox is back on full power. It's like I've been in the dark for weeks and somebody's flicked the lights on, been watching a black-and-white programme and it's just gone into colour.

I fancy a quick one but I'll settle for a drink. Uh ho, yes. Richard did that one earlier. How they all laughed. I'll remember that. Keep it for a rainy day, then I'll do it and that way they'll like me. Think I'm a damn fine funny fellow.

I'm not strictly, strictly not allowed. It said that on the paper that came with the pills too. *It is strongly advised that the patient avoid alcohol.*

You can bet your bottom bollock the cow read, learnt and inwardly digested that part. You can also bet your top testicle if it'd said anything good, anything of benefit like *It is strongly advised the patient be tossed off twice daily and then given a steak sandwich* she'd have ignored that completely and said doctors don't know everything, clean the bogs, get your own tea and there's more protein in a tin of beans anyway.

So, a drink it is then, and there's such a fine selection of hostelry in this town where I live – if indeed you care to call it living – that I hardly know where to begin.

The Market Tavern in the market? Too crowded.

The Railway down by the railway? Too noisy. The place shakes five times an hour and anyway it's run by a pair of arse-gardeners. If you drop your wallet in there, kick it away, kick it away.

The Riverside by the riverside? No, definitely not the Riverside. Last time I was there, sipping a chilled orange crush, soaking up the summer sun, basking in the splendours of the beer garden and watching a gaggle of toddlers in the children's play area systematically vandalising a swing and see-saw, a stiff surfaced amongst the water lilies, and like they say, one dark-green rotting corpse can spoil your whole day.

The Bowling Green by the bowling green? No, nothing even faintly green today, thank you.

So?

None of the above. Think I'll patronise the RegNancy Hotel this fine autumn noon. Honour them with my presence. Anyway, Dogs Are Allowed and it's the nearest.

The outside of the place is painted matt white with wobbly Tudor beams daubed on in lumpy gloss black – which looks dead wrong on a flat-roofed '50s building.

The name is silly. If I've told Reg once I'll have told him twice – it just does not work. Him, his wife Nancy and their hotel. Reg says it's a play on words. It is a play on words. Of sorts at any rate, but really not a very good one.

If it were a Regency building, if it was a proper hotel, not just a boozer that did the occasional B & B, and if Nancy changed her name to Ency it'd be spot on, a cockbird as they say round here. Reg says it's too late to change it now, the name of the boozer I mean, as it's so well known.

He's got a point there has Reg. It is well known. All over the local area. The stupidest name around.

Reg says he originally got the idea after visiting a greasy spoon in Retford. Me'n'u, they called it. Reg thought that was right clever. I rest my case.

Nancy's one of those women. One of those dippy tarts who think it's a good idea to shave off the eyebrows then draw them back on again a full two inches further up the forehead. She looks permanently shocked does Nancy and she dresses with a Spanish feel. Gold slip-ons, tight red pants with brocade up the sides, thin frilly top, long black hair tied too hard back, bright-green eyeshadow, bright-blue jewellery. Colourful Senior Service Señora caught completely unawares by belligerent bull. Don't get me wrong, Nancy's got a good-quality pair of castanets lurking under that frilly pink blouse, a decent set of pins for her age, a reasonably tight little rear, pretty brown eyes and a sexy laugh. She's a good laugh an' all. First time I ever went in there she introduced Reg as her first husband and stood me a drink.

It's just a pity she's got a face like a cow's arse.

Reg has affectionate eyes – they spend most of the time just looking at each other. It doesn't do to mock the afflicted, I know. What would Richard say? It is not politically correct, Bruce, it is not appropriate, to rip the piss out of a tragically cross-eyed man. And he's right.

I shouldn't.

But it is fun.

Reg wears maroon V-necked pullovers, white drip-dry shirts, top-buttoned, but no tie. He sports cream slacks in the summer, black ones in the winter, and, when it's really hot, and Nancy's not looking, Reg parks his shoes in the fridge.

Reg is red, not in his political complexion, I've no idea what Reg's politics are – and I'm prepared to bet strong money Reg hasn't either – but in his fizzog, his actual complexion.

When I start to think about it and if I stop to think about it, Reg's redness rivets me and once I've started I can't stop. I can't even begin to imagine how he ended up that colour. Did he start as a little pink baby and finish as a great big fire-engine-faced goit? Did he flush beetroot with embarrassment one fine but blustery day just as the wind changed, or did somebody once compliment him upon his pinkness and our Reg simply decided to accentuate his best feature to its grotesque and illogical conclusion?

Ladies and gentleman, boys and girls, cats and kittens, rabbits and cavies, hamsters and gerbils. Why the fuck is Reg so red?

RegNancy Hotel.

First thing in the a.m., upstairs kitchen.

You can picture the scene.

Nancy at the table leafing through the post. Reg at the stove, staring excitedly into a catering-sized pan of water.

Reg watches as the lower layer of water stiffens and begins to move. Tiny pinprick bubbles appear on the base of the pan, grow bigger and explode on to the surface. After two minutes the water's rolling, folding in on itself and fizzing into steam.

Nancy looks up from page 8 of the new Innovations Catalogue. She makes a mental note to order a new kind of sink tidy, a spin-off from the space race, and checks the kitchen clock, a quartz-controlled, laser-powered job, a spin-off from the arms race and also featured in the Innovations Catalogue.

'Ready, darling?'

'Yep.'

Nancy seizes Reg by the loose skin on the nape of his neck and plunges his face deep into the pan.

Reg feels like screaming as he feels the superheated tap water bite deep into the bags under his eyes and etch into the creases behind his ears, but half a life-time's experience has taught him to keep his mouth clamped tight shut.

Nancy checks the clock.

'Fifteen seconds gone, Reg, shall we give it another ten?'

'Uh, Uh. Uh, Uh. Uh,' Reg grunts. Which means *Yes, thank you, darling, that would be lovely.*

By now Reg's left leg's trembling so hard he's kicking the sliding pan drawer at the base of the oven and his clenched fists are twitching like a couple of spaccas against his sides.

Nancy checks the clock again, gives him a couple more seconds for luck and lets go.

Reg staggers over to the table, slumps into a chair

and sits in silence while Nancy pats his face dry with a clean teatowel. Nancy leans over and fishes a folded card strip and a small oblong mirror from her handbag.

'Look, Reg,' she says, scanning the paint chart. 'You were Flaming June yesterday, but today you're even darker. Volcanic at least.'

She hands Reg the mirror so he can have a look.

'Thanks for that, love,' Reg says, smoothing back his hair. 'That's right good. We've time for a coffee before we open up, and there's half a pan of boiling water going begging. It'd be a right shame to waste it.'

'Waste it, Reg. Please. We can't drink that. That's a horrible thought. I'll put the kettle on.'

Eeeyuk. Can you imagine that, making coffee with the same water Reg's just had his face boiled in? Beef tea maybe but . . .

'Bruce, what on earth are you doing standing out here in the dark?'

Shit, it's Linda and she's right, it is dark. How the hell did that happen?

'I was just thinking. I was thinking of taking a walk into town.'

'Well, it's too late for that now, the shops'll all be shutting and anyway it's teatime. Why don't you go tomorrow instead? If you'll just see me into the garage and lock up, I'll get the tea on.'

'What we having?'

'Beans on toast, Bruce, quick and easy, and more protein than a piece of steak.'

'Some fuckin' day off, I've 'ad,' Gary says, leaning into his third pint. He pauses, then necks the lot and slaps a two-pound coin on the bar.

Reg pulls him another and hands him the change without saying anything.

High up over the bar there's a telly fixed on a metal bracket. When it was new the telly was neat, white and contemporary. Now it's scruffy, dated and the colour of old teeth.

Since the roadworks started her life's been a living hell.

'It started last night, pissin' out water, all over kitchen floor. Pumpin' out it were. Went down Burlack's first thing this mornin', choice of two, seventy-five notes apiece. Well, Kay – it were spin speed that did it – said she'd have the fast 'un, said they'd deliver's afternoon and scrap old 'un. Did they fuck. Bin stuck in all day waitin' for the cunts.'

The noise is terrible and there's mud everywhere.

'So anyway, I've said to 'er when she gets back from your place, Kay, I've bin stuck in all fuckin' day waitin' for them cunts to deliver and I've phoned the fuckers twice and now they've said it'll 'ave to be tomorrow so

I'm off down RegNancy for a pint. Think I'll try another one in there, Reg.'

A council spokesman said they are monitoring the situation.

'An' another thing, we've a fuckin' mystery in our 'ouse. Yer know the glass plate? Fits in bottom of microwave? Can't find the cunt anywhere. She thinks I've bust it and not said but I'a'n't.'

And finally, a Worksop man is planning to shave off his beard for charity. Christa Ackroyd went to ask him why.

'Can we 'ave that fuckin' telly off, Reg? Nobody's watchin' the cunt, tha comes down 'ere for a bit a peace, not to listen to that shite.'

Reg comes out from behind the bar.

He drags a chair away from one of cast-framed, marble-topped tables and parks it under the telly. He climbs on to the chair, steadies himself with his left hand against its curved back and presses the on button off with his right forefinger. Reg replaces the chair and settles himself back.

Back behind the bar.

'Better?'

'Marvellous.'

'Anyway, like I were saying, got a right busy day on tomorrow, pulled out wi' work we are. Fifty dwarfs in mornin', fifty more in afternoon.'

'Gnomes, Gary, gnomes.'

'Yer what?'

'Gnomes. They're not dwarfs, they're gnomes.'

'Well, now then, Brucie me ol'. Ah've been studying on that un. Now listen while I tells yer summat. My dwarfs, right? Short fuckers, big pointy fuckin' 'ats, cheeky little fuckin' faces?'

'Yes, but . . .'

'But fuckin' nothin'. Think on. Film, cartoon it is, Snow White an' t' Seven Dwarfs, they call it, not, *not*, Snow White an' t' Seven Fuckin' Gnomes. All this fuckin' time you've bin callin' me, all this fuckin' time, callin' me for sayin' fuckin' dwarfs an' I've bin fuckin' right all a fuckin' long.'

'Yes, Gary, but . . .'

'You fuck off, yer fuckin' cunt.'

Just as he calls me cunt Gary cracks me a big daft grin. Round here cunt is shorthand for my very good friend. It's when they call you pal you need to watch it.

I like it here. You can fit in. Get yourself a drink, nod, smile, say the odd thing, drink your drink and feel included.

'What's this fuckin' box on counter wi' teddy on it?'

Nancy pokes her head up over the bar. She's been down there the whole time, sorting the softs, counting the crisps, marshalling the mixers.

'It's a swear box, Gary.'

Nancy fills a clean ashtray with water and puts it down for Bruno. She helps herself to a Britvic 55, takes a sip, pulls a face then adds a double vodka.

'A fuckin' what?'

'A swear box, Gary, it's for Children in Need. Fs are fifty pence, cs a pound. You owe us fifteen quid.'

'Fuckin' 'ell.'

'Fifteen pounds fifty.'

'Anyway, how's yerself, Captain? Linda let you out, 'as she?'

'I'm fine, Gary, thank you. I'd thought you'd never ask. I'm out on an errand actually but I appear to have forgotten what it is.'

'Can you 'ear this cunt, Nancy? From same place as rest of us, this 'un, 'ave you 'eard how he fuckin' talks?'

'Seventeen quid.'

'Sorry, Gary, I can't help it.'

'You're all right, Bruce, only messin'. Whisky?'

'Go on then. Thanks.'

I call into the paper shop on the way home. Two packets of extra-strong mints should do the trick. I follow the scar they left when they laid cable TV, veering off every now and again and up people's driveways.

I don't feel right.

More tired than anything.

I stop outside Just Tyres, lean up against the chipped yellow railing and roll a fag. There's a splash of paint on the asphalt I've never noticed before. It looks just like a spinal column.

I get down on my hands and knees to have a better look. A hand on my shoulder and a couple of lads in

Just Tyres overalls just staring. Rebecca helps me up and dusts me down.

'I thought it was you, Bruce. I've been bipping you for ages.'

She opens the passenger door of her red Metro and waits while I get in. Rebecca goes round the front of the car, opens the driver's door, slides in, starts the engine, flicks off the hazards and indicates left.

And as she waits for a break in the traffic I watch the fingers of her left hand sliding up and down the chrome shaft of the gear lever and the cup of her palm swivelling across the smooth black bulb. I knew it. Gagging, absolutely gagging. Bet if I suggested it now she'd drive us out to the country, park up in some secluded spot, peel off her . . .

'You all right, Bruce?'

'Yes, just tired.'

'What were you doing down there?'

'Just looking at something.'

'You looked passed out to me, flat on your face, you were. Are you sure you're OK?'

'Yes, really. I'm just tired.'

'Look, why don't you come back to mine. I'll make you a coffee and you can wash your face, it's all grubby. Then you can just walk home and Linda won't be worried.'

Here we go. This is it. Come back to mine for a coffee, brackets slippery animal fuck. Not very original but who's bothered. I knew it, I flipping knew it.

'I've just been at your place, in fact I've been there all day helping Linda. She said you'd be out all day, see if you could spot some holly and get Bruno from under her feet. By the way, where is Bruno?'

It's a wild old night, wind crashing through the trees, rattling the sashes, sucking out the chimneys and nothing on the telly. Only sex. All that's ever on these days. I hate it, hate to see them at it. How do they think it makes us feel, all us that aren't getting any and no prospect of getting any.

Give a starving woman a cookbook. In between commercial breaks show me a well-stacked blonde getting fucked from here to kingdom come. And they always come. Loud American sex, they have, noisy transatlantic orgasms. Trent and Chuck and Buck, bright-blue eyes and bodies like trucks. Giving it to women with perfect teeth and names like cars.

Linda's out. Gone to the pictures with Kay. *Personal Services*, I think, unless Kay's told her something I really hope she hasn't. There was a note waiting on the kitchen table when I got back from my coffee and a wash at Rebecca's. So I read it, read the words, that's how I know. *Gone to the flicks with Kay* (Personal Services!), *get your own tea, don't forget your tablets*. Then a single x.

I'm going to the doghouse when she gets back. I do think about killing myself sometimes, just for something to do, and only ever out of spite. There's a perfect place in the upstairs lav. Throw a rope over that beam and lock the door. Ascend the throne then abdicate. The perfect way to make them notice, feel bad, give me another chance.

I read somewhere hanging gives you a hard-on, and that would be just typical. Best one of my life probably and me far too dead to see it.

You know what I feel like doing now, what I really feel like doing?

Take myself up to the top landing, proceed in an orderly fashion through the attic into next door then work down. Smash every single piece of tat, grind every last priceless article of Edwardian junk to a powder then roll myself up in a rug and wait for the fun to start. Bruce Glasscock centre stage. For one night only, all eyes on me.

I make a coffee, don't forget my tablets, take my tablets and go up to my room. I switch on the clock radio, read my book for a bit then nod off.

I wake with a jolt. Eleven thirty-five.

Voices downstairs and Bruno thumping his tail against the radiators. Footsteps up the stairs and then the door eases open. Oh Christ, here we go, one giant shitstorm headed directly this way.

'Me and Kay are having a nightcap and I thought you might fancy a little glass.'

'Thanks.'

'Are you all right now, Bruce?'

'Er. Yes, Linda.'

'We met up with Gary after the flicks and he told us all about what happened, about how you dealt with the druggie in the RegNancy.'

'The who?'

'The druggie, the lad who came in and tried to steal the swearbox.'

'The swearbox?'

'Yes, Gary told us all about it, how you took it back and chased the lad outside. Sounds like you were quite the hero. Gary said you were a bit shaken up after, though. He's given Bruno his tea and we've just picked him up. He's ever so glad to be home, you should see him.'

'Ah. Good.'

'And thanks ever so for finding all that holly and mistletoe too – fancy it all being up behind Kenton Precast. Gary says when we're ready for it he'll bring it over to Clumber in the firm's pick-up and he's bringing us some dwarfs for the raffle.'

'Clumber?'

'You know, the Duke's study. Don't tell me you've forgotten, Bruce. Regional HQ, the Duke's study by the stables? Where we're having the Victorian Christmas Fayre?'

'Ah yes. Sorry, Lindy, I'm a bit tired.'

She runs her hand through my hair then kisses me lightly on the forehead.

'Night night.'

When Richard comes in next morning he looks worried.

'There's three or four slates sticking out the front lawn – just seen 'em as I came up the path. Storm last night must've fetched 'em off. Cracker, wasn't it?'

'Oh God,' Linda says, 'more expense, just what we need.'

'What? Won't the Trust just send someone? It's only a five-minute job.'

'Yes, they will, Richard, but that someone'll be a builder registered with the Trust and five-minute job or not, he'll charge an arm and a leg. Only have to hear the magic words English Trust and pound signs light up in their eyes – and it comes straight out of my budget.'

'Your budget?'

'I'll take you through this properly when we've got a bit more time but . . .'

'I.e. never.'

'Shutup, Bruce. Every property has a budget for small repairs, photocopier hire, volunteers' expenses, what have you. Major repairs are paid directly by the Trust. A couple of minor repairs can make a nasty hole in it, set us right back. That's why we fundraise. Sometimes, say, if it's a major project like William's greenhouse and his cacti collection, if we can raise half, the Trust'll stump up the rest – matchfunding they call it.'

'Yes, that's right, they pay half and then take all the credit, the whole lot. That long-haired ponce Simon appears in local press, on local telly, takes all the credit and gets a pay rise – even though he despises this place.'

'Bruce. I wish you wouldn't talk about the Trust like that – they've been good to us, even put a roof over our head.'

'Yeah, anyway,' Richard says. 'Meanwhile, back at the ranch. The roof. Is it a new roof?'

'Of course it isn't a new roof. Don't be ridiculous, man. This is an English Trust property.'

'Actually, Bruce, it is meant to be a new roof. It was down in all the plans as being a new roof when I took over and I've never really understood that. It looks like an old one to me too, and there's no need to speak to Richard like that.'

'Have you ever been up in the loft space?'

'Yes, a few times, Richard. Why?'

'Is it felted?'

'What?'

'When you look up can you see the backs of the slates or is there a layer of black stuff? Like stiff oily fabric.'

'There's definitely fabric. In my mum's house you could see daylight through all the chinks between the tiles and here you can't. It's pitch black. I remember thinking that.'

'Right. So it's felted – so they'll have replaced the latts as well. What they'll have done is strip off all the slates, dead carefully, felted, re-latted, redone all the leadwork, valleys, soakers, flashings and stuff and then put the old slates back on with new copper nails. I did the offshot on my place a couple of years back – it took me ages but I did it. The slates are generally fine unless they've delaminated – it's always the nails that go. Nail sickness they call it.

'Anyway, what I'm trying to say is that if you can get hold of a ladder I'll do it if you want. Don't think I'll even need a crawler. I'll check, but I reckon the slates you've lost are all from the verges where the roof tips into the gutter. If they've done it right they'll have hipped the last row up a bit for ventilation and it's always those ones that the wind picks up. Good job they all hit the lawn, eh? Copper strap under each one should do nicely.'

Linda looks a bit taken aback so I seize my chance. I've been top dog around here for the last two days, Sunny Jim, and I most certainly am not losing pole position now, not to some jumped-up little gobshite who's suddenly the world's greatest expert on everything.

Don't think you'll need a crawler, no, you're perfectly correct on that score, Richard, you won't need a crawler:

A. because you are a fucking crawler and

B. because you will not be fucking doing it.

'And since when did you know so much about the subject, Richard? Since when were you such an expert and since when did you think that we'd even consider letting a volunteer loose on this place? I bet your landlord was delighted with you, wasn't he, hacking at his roof? If you'd have been my tenant I know what I'd have done, I'd have given you your fucking marching orders.'

'Right,' he says, getting up from his chair. 'Fine. Actually, it's my own house so I don't have a landlord. Anyway I've got stuff to be getting on with. Super talking to you, Bruce.'

He goes into the office and slams the door behind him.

Linda gets up too.

'How many times, how many times, Bruce, have I told you not to swear at the volunteers? Now isn't it about time you took Bruno out? And make sure you fetch him back this time.'

'Lindy, I just thought . . .'

She holds up her palm like a policeman on point duty.

'Don't.'

'But, Linda . . .'

'Just go, will you, Bruce.'

A long time ago, I made a lifestyle choice – as they'd say in Linda's magazines. I decided that the best policy was to pretend to know fuck all. It got me through school, it got me through the army and ever since then it's being getting me in the shit.

Bruno trots along in front of me on a slack leash. He stops at the drain and he shits. I reach into my pocket for a plastic bag, but this morning it is not required and neither am I. Not this or any other morning.

It's cold today. It's a cold old planet and every morning I cheer myself up with the thought that I'm another day nearer death.

I've seen the world and I didn't like it. Postings all over the show. They wake you up in Malta, they wake you up in Germany, they wake you up in Cyprus, they wake you up in the Westgate training centre, Rotherham and it's always the same: two sheets, four blankets, one locker, one cabinet, one bedside mat. Blanco, sweat and shit. Stick man if you're lucky, guard duty if you're not. Weekend pass, evenings in the NAAFI, nights in the guardroom, afternoons in the butts. Five in the clip and one up the spout.

I stop where our gravel drag merges into the tarmac of the proper road, fish in my pocket for fags – raw materials for the construction of – and they're not there. I knew they wouldn't be, I didn't feel right when I left the house. I'll have left them on the kitchen table. Only take a minute.

I loop Bruno's lead over the front gate, creep back up the path, round the back, in through the kitchen door, and there they are just where I thought they'd be. Linda's in the office with Richard and it sounds like Rebecca's in there too. I pull the door to quietly as I can and set off back down the path. Bruno's barking and as I come round the side of the house I see it's because Kay's making a fuss of him.

'Morning, Kay.'

'Bruce.'

'Kay, will you thank Gary when you see him, tell him I owe him one.'

'Tell him yourself. You know the score and you know I know. Me an' Gary had a row last night on your account, him covering up for you like that. You, a grown man and with Linda so busy, it's pathetic. And another thing, Linda told me how you saved the day with the garage key. I needed some fresh cotton waste out of there yesterday. I used the key off the back of the cellar door and it worked first time, so I know your little game and I know for a fact that you've done it before.'

I watch as she stomps up the path, cuts across our garden and lets herself into the Hays House next door.

I keep thinking she might turn, smile at me like it's all right again or maybe just give me a half-one to show she's seen the funny side. But she doesn't.

I crouch and smooth out Bruno's ears, shine his coat with the flat of my hand. As I straighten up I notice Stony – first time I've had a proper look at him for a couple of days – and as I go to kick him I realise he looks different.

Poor little Stony. His head's come off, a flat white plateau of fresh concrete levelling off his shoulders. You wouldn't think a good frost could do that to a concrete dwarf's neck but it does and you wouldn't think that one small thing could brighten your whole day but it does, and I laugh until tears run down my face.

I remember once when I was a kid and I was fed up or bored or in trouble for something and Mum was dragging me round the shops with the Back to Skool displays in the windows – which they put in with the express purpose of spoiling the summer holidays before they've even hardly started – I saw a woman slam her hand so hard in a car door that I was still laughing when Mum slapped me the third time.

Back down the drive again. I lean up against a concrete lamp-post which is still firmly in one piece, and was most likely not manufactured by Kenton Precast, and notice there's a notice fixed to it with red cable ties.

No risk, big rewards. Seriously increase your income. I trap Bruno's lead with my foot, roll a fag and smoke it.

I'd better find Gary. Thank him for saving my skin when I got pissed and forgot the dog. He's a sharp tack is Gary, a man's man – doesn't tell the ladies what they don't need to know – and he sorted out the holly. I'll buy him a pint, tell him about Kay, beg him to forgive me. Maybe not that last part, but get him a pint at least.

I could tell him about Stony.

T welve o'clock.

High noon already and it doesn't seem properly
light yet. Cold, grey, freezing – no weather to speak of.
Gary'll be in the Navigation waiting for his first batch
of gnomes to set. If I cut along the cut I'll catch him.

I like walking the canal, you see the backside of
everything and you feel hidden, out of the way, as if
you're burrowing just under the skin, drifting the slow
lymph of this depressing little town. Bruno loves it
down here too, lots of interesting smells for him to fuss
over, uprights for him to piss up.

There's a few blokes fishing the first turning basin we
come to and Bruno charges over to say hello. That's the
thing about dogs, they break the ice, all you have to do
is go over, retrieve them, say a few words and before
you know it you're chatting to a total stranger.

By the time I reach the Navigation it's almost one
and I know more about carbon-fibre roach poles,
elasticated top-threes, semi-barbless hooks and Van
den Eyde groundbait than I ever thought possible. I
used to fish myself, loved it when I was a kid, but it all
seems a bit too technical these days.

Soon as I push open one half of the tatty mahogany

swing doors to the public bar I spot Gary in the far corner with one of his workmates, holding forth loudly about the latest advances and up-to-the-minute refinements in Toetector technology.

The Navigation's a proper pub, a real workman's boozer, packed all day and deserted in the evenings. In through the door and it's a straight choice, lounge on the left, public on the right.

The public's not been altered since the place was built – tiled floor, tiled walls, long benches, scarred oak tables. Some joker with time on his hands and a chisel in his bag has set a double-six domino perfectly flush into the surface of the table nearest the Gents. In pride of place over the bar there's a gilt-framed photo of Gary, smart as paint in his wedding suit, grey silk topper, buttonhole, waistcoat, shiny black shoes, trousers round his ankles, being sick into a red plastic bucket.

No idea what it's like in the lounge – never set foot in there, nobody ever has.

I get myself a Scotch and a pint for Gary and go over. Gary introduces me to his mate Mick and makes a fuss of Bruno.

'See these fuckers, Bruce,' he says, banging an industrial-sized pair of trainers on to the table and forcing Mick to lurch forward in order to save his whole pint from spillage.

'Guess what these fuckers are? Bet thee fuckin' can't.'

'Would they be Toetectors by any chance, Gary?' Mick starts laughing and spills a bit more.

''Ow did thee guess?'

'It's all you ever talk about, Gary, plus they weigh about half a ton each and that box on the seat next you says *Toetectors* in big blue letters.'

'Yeah, but if you 'an't known that would thee ever have guessed? I mean honestly, yer clever cunt, would thee ever have taken these fuckin' trainers for fuckin' Toetectors, they just look like fuckin' trainers, don't they?'

'Yeah, Gary. Correct,' Mick says. 'But only the kind of fuckin' trainers the fuckin' diddy-fuckin' men'd wear down fuckin' treacle mines at fuckin' Knotty fuckin' Ash. Look at fuckin' toes on 'em, like fuckin' cricket balls, they are.'

'Yeah, well,' Gary says and he looks genuinely hurt. 'I think they're fuckin' great.'

A high-pitch siren blares from a low concrete shed just by the pub.

Gary necks his pint, picks up the pint I've just fetched him and necks that too. I don't know how he does it – if I had to drink two pints of water at that speed I'd most likely chuck, but Gary just opens his throat and down it goes.

'Hi fuckin' ho,' Gary says, 'better get back to it. Come back wi' us, Bruce, and I'll show you fuckin' ivy or whatever it fuckin' is.'

Mick gets himself another pint, Gary says he'll see him later, then we pick our way along a muddy track down the side of the fence out on to a concrete drive and in through the double wire gates of Kenton Precast.

Gary stops off inside the gates and has a quick word with a bloke leaning against a wooden hut. The bloke nods at me and I nod back. We cross a flat concrete yard. It looks like a municipal cemetery, a herd of concrete donkeys with panniers for bedding plants, battalions of precast gnomes, miles of sectioned balustrade, enough bird baths to clean the entire sparrow population of the British Isles, piles of copings, stacks of fake riven slabs, a reef of huge concrete seashells and a whole shoe shop's worth of oversized concrete boots even heavier than Gary's Toetectors.

When I've finally managed to drag Bruno away from the last of the gnomes I tell Gary about Stony, and after Gary's stopped laughing we go round the back of the factory and stand on a scrubby bit of ground. It's covered in holly bushes, some with berries, some without, and there's even some variegated stuff that Linda'll be really chuffed about.

'This lot do yer, Captain?'

'Yes, Gary, thanks, and thanks for yesterday, you saved my bacon, saved me a lot of trouble. I owe you one.'

'You owe me more than one, yer fuckin' cunt, yer owe me 'bout five fuckin' 'undred.'

Gary undoes the belt on his jeans and unbuttons his flies and just for a second I catch sight of his penis. Enormous. Like a baby's arm holding an apple. Christ, I'd love to see that thing when it's angry. Imagine that. Pumped up, sliding in and out of Kay. Gary turns his back.

'Fuckin' 'ell, them last two've gone right fuckin' thru me,' he says, steam rising up around his knees.

I turn my back, unzip my flies and do the same. And it must be the pills. I have one of my moments. Bruno sits by me on a slack leash. I have a real feeling of time and where we are in it. I see myself and I see Gary, I see us both from up above, see us back to back like we were about to fight a duel with our schlontz – me with a kid's water-pistol, Gary with a .88 German field gun – perfectly at ease and pouring piss into the broken ground.

'Gary, there's something else I need to tell you. About Kay and last year,' I hear myself say, and I'm wondering what that bloke down there who looks a lot like me is going to say to Gary next and how long it'll take for an ambulance to get here.

'Shut it, cunt,' Gary says, and reaches his arm up behind him so it brushes my back.

'It's done wi'. Don't ever fuckin' do it again.'

Little animals. Fuck me, little little animals are everywhere. It's December for fuck's sake and those fucking little animals are still fucking everywhere. Slugs on the path, woodlice under the leaves and worms slithering in the earth. Ants.

When I get back home I feel surprised. I'm back. Hey, hey, I'm back, and did you miss me while I was away? No, I don't think you fucking did, did you?

I'm sat on the back step. I roll a fag, set light to the cunt and smoke it.

The air smells like snow. I remember the first time I kissed her. She cut through me, then the drinks cut me in half. I put a ring on her finger and brushed back her hair. I am, I am not a freak. Somehow I lost connection, somehow I lost my way. Mind like a sewer, memory like a sieve.

I swore I'd always be with her, keep her safe, learn a trade, do the washing up. One stinking squaddie house after another – never our own. Put the paper up with drawing pins, take it down again, fill the holes with toothpaste, move on.

She takes the ring off now. Leaves it on the sill by the sink. Piles up the dishes. Linda does the washing up.

Gary does the washing up, Kay's not up to his standards, he says. I check for Bruno. He's back. He's with me and we're both here. We're both back.

I let myself in the back door. It hinges on the left. Three brass ones with a steel washer in each of the knuckles. I twist the egg-shaped brass knob anti-clockwise, the sneck unlatches. I ease the door away from me and watch as the draught-excluder brushes on the bottom sweep a quadrant of super-clean floor back into the kitchen. I step in.

Richard's in the exhibition room working through a rail of William's clothes. He turns the suits inside out, then vacuums the fabric through a mesh exactly as Kay's shown him, and exactly as it says in the Trust manual of housekeeping. He's got the dustette on a strap slung over his shoulder, like some sort of space cadet. He's singing. He thinks no one can hear him over the whoosh of the vacuum.

'We used to have a lot in com-mon and now we're ju-ust the same.'

'What's that, Richard?' and he looks up. He looks surprised and a bit embarrassed – he can't have heard me come in.

'Oh yer know, nothing, Bruce, it's a song, just a song.'

'You look like a spaceman with that thing over your shoulder.'

'Oh yeah,' he says, 'dusty blue serge strikes the planet Hays. Fluff threatens the earth. Junior Jetpants to the rescue.'

'So how are we finding it at the Hays?'

'Fine. I really like it here.'

'Good man, good man. So how's your love life, soldier?'

'Oh, yer know,' he says, and he looks surprised and a bit sad.

'No girlfriend then? I take it you're not queer, not a bloody dinnerbasher, are we, Richard?'

'Oh, no,' he says, 'I'm not. I'm not gay, but thanks for asking, Bruce. I've got a girlfriend all right, like I said before. Clare – but she's away, she's in Scotland on a course. You've met her actually, remember? When we first came round the house?'

'Christ, Richard, you lucky dog! She was the one with the tits? Oh sweet Jesus! The blonde with the massive top bollocks? She's your girl? You're boning that?'

'No, Bruce, that's her friend Sam. Clare's the one with the long dark hair.'

'So how big are Clare's tits?'

'Er, normal, I suppose.'

'Bet they're still nice though. Big enough for you, are they, eh? Nice warm handful?'

'Er, yeah. Yes, they are nice, Bruce. Clare is nice, very nice actually. Anyway she's away for a while and I miss her lots.'

He turns his back, snatches another suit down from the rail and switches on the dustette.

Sam. So that was her name. Short for Samantha, I suppose. Bloody hell, do I remember her? The young Diana Dors had nothing on Sam. The four of us, me and Sam and Sam's outstanding pair of tits, were getting along so well, so famously, I forgot to take anybody's money and I completely forgot the intro-duction in the exhibition room, which I know off pat. I personally escorted her next door and saw her back to her car after they'd finished the tour, and after I'd slapped the bonnet and sent them on their way I spent half an hour in the bathroom, to absolutely no fucking avail, and the rest of the day in the doghouse.

'Never mind, Richard,' I say, then realise he can't hear me over the noise of the dustette.

'I'm sure Kay'll let you have a bash when I've finished with her,' I say to the back of his over-educated head.

'I saw ants in the front garden today. It's December for fuck's sake and I saw ants. What we all need reet now is a reet good frost. Burn off all the fuckin' bugs. Not cold are you, Richard? You poncy little college cunt.'

You want to change yer butcher. Get some meat on thee bones. Neck some shit that sticks to yer ribs. Next time you're beating your dick on the edge of the basin, Sunny Jim, waiting for your lady love to return from Jockland, just you think about that.

'Just you fucking think about that.'

Can't stop thinking about that bloody tree. In 1905 William senior planted it slap bang in the middle of the front garden and it's been a pain in the arse ever since.

Every single morning Lindy has me out there scratching round it with the rake. The pink blossoms fall and go brown. Linda says it's unsightly, her perfect green lawn spoilt by crispy brown scurf, plus it's the first thing the visitors will see as they come up the path to the Hays House and it gives a bad impression. So I rake it all up.

The fruits form, ripen and drop off. Linda says you mustn't eat them, not ornamental cherry; not sure whether that's true or not, but we don't, eat them, I mean. The wasps eat them though, love 'em, they do, they all get piss-arsed, then they get angry. Linda says we can't have that, have the visitors stung to buggery by drunken little jaspers, although it sounds pretty damn good to me. So I rake up the fruits.

The leaves yellow, brown and hit the deck. Autumn fucking tints or not it makes a bloody mess, does nature, and it's me that has to deal with the damn things. And just like the blossoms and the fruit the

121

leaves haven't the common decency or the common sense to drop off wholesale, oh no, no, no, that twisted little sod of a tree likes to take its time, just shed a few today, thank you, just enough to keep Bruce – uncrowned king of the meaningless little job – preoccupied, and dispense with maybe a few more tomorrow, thirty or forty the day after and some other odd number the day after that.

I was out there yesterday first thing in the morning. Fetched the rake from the garage, got a bag from the kitchen and set to. Ended up on my hands and knees picking up the stragglers, crawling around like an idiot in front of that bloody tree like I was worshipping the wooden bastard.

Fifteen minutes later, job done, as the scouts used to say. Leaned back against the old trunk, looking up into the branches, rolled a fag and relaxed. Just then, just as I spark up and take the first drag, the exact same bloody leaf that I'm staring at decides its time has come and spirals down on to the immaculate green lawn.

Fuck it, I think, who's the boss around here, me or this tree, or even that bloody leaf I'll leave till tomorrow. Hah! leaf it till tomorrow, uh ho, yes! Every one's a coconut, Glasscock, you are indeed on good form this merry morn. So that cheers me up a bit. *Mañana* it is.

Kay comes up the path and from down here on the ground I get a much better view of her legs than usual.

'You've missed one,' says the bitch.

I wish I was blind sometimes, I really do. So I wouldn't see the mess this world is in, trees festooned with litter, rusty bikes shoved down the sides of collapsing sheds, flat roofs repaired with polythene, cracks in the pavements, chewing gum, dog shit, leaves.

Can't sleep for thinking about the fuckers. Only ten leaves left, dead but clinging on to the top branches for dear life. Survived the storm and everything did those obstinate ten, and they'll probably time it so they fall on the morning of the Hays Christmas meal, I bet they will, just as snotty Simon from Trust HQ ponces up the path.

Well, I won't have it. Do you hear me, you dried-up little perishers? I will not have it.

I go down to the kitchen, turn off the alarm, get myself a coffee, roll and ignite first fag of the day. Three o'clock in the a.m., flat calm, nearly a full moon, Bruno sound asleep. I fetch my green hunter wellies from the cellar head, pull them on and tuck my pyjama bottoms neatly into the tops.

Out the back door, down the path, out into the road. Next Edwardian semi up is where we want to be, soldier. Open the front gate nice and quiet, that's right – easy does it – and step on to the lawn. There she blows. Twisting skywards the centre of the greens-ward, our very dear friend the ornamental fucking tree.

Right.

Legs apart, deep breath. Grasp trunk firmly with both hands . . . and wait, wait for it, Glasscock . . . shake. That's right, soldier, rock it back and forth nice and steady . . . and halt.

Oh yes. Three or four that time, fluttering down to earth in the pale moonlight. Like Gary would say, job is a fuckin' good'un. We are cooking with gas, are we not.

Well done, that man. Good start. Same procedure this time, soldier, jerkier movements if you can and . . .

'Bruce, Bruce, is that you down there?'

Shit.

. . . and shake.

'Bruce, what on earth do you think you're playing at – it's gone three in the morning.'

'Just doing a spot of gardening, dear, nothing to worry about.'

. . . and shake.

Linda opens her bedroom window a bit wider and leans right out. The moon's so bright that even from next door's garden I still get a smashing view of her tits.

. . . and shake.

'Bruce. What are you doing?'

'I'm just trying, I am just trying, Linda, to get it over with.'

I go back to bed but I don't sleep. Soon as it gets light I take Bruno out. Bruno trots along in front of me on a slack leash. It's a beautiful morning. I round the front of our, of Lindy's, house and scan the tree in the Hays front garden. Naked, absolutely stark, not a stitch, perfect. Nice work, soldier. Well done, that man.

Richard knocks the back door and doesn't wait. He waltzes in all smiles. He's wearing one of those bobble hats without a bobble on them.

'Yo,' he says, and gives me and Lindy the double thumbs-up.

'Uh?'

'Yo,' he says again. 'It means like hey, bro's, how's it hanging in the er, hood.'

'Uh?'

'It means good morning, Bruce, Linda, how are things generally about the old place?'

'So why were you talking like that, Richard?'

'When I wear this hat, Linda, when I wear this hat I'm black, maybe not young or gifted but black anyway.'

'Well, don't wear it then, we don't want any bloody niggers in this house.'

'Bruce, there's no need for that. Remember our little chat about PC?'

'No, not really, dear. Anyway they call each other that, heard two of 'em at it in the precinct yesterday.'

'Do they?'

'Yes, my darling Lindy, they do.'

Got you this time, I'm thinking. Got you both.

'So, young man, since you're the world's greatest expert on what I can and cannot say in my own bloody kitchen . . .'

'Bruce . . .'

'Sorry, Lindy, in my own, in our kitchen, then how the hell do you explain that? They call each other nigger, we call 'em nigger.'

'Oh gawd,' Richard says. 'It's a bit early in the morning for all this, but . . .'

'Well, you bloody started it.'

'Yes, I know, Bruce, and I wish I'd not now, but the reason they can and we can't is because, well, it's because when they say it . . .'

'You mean nigger.'

'When they say it it's like they're taking that term of abuse back off us and by using it themselves it's not going to hurt them any more. I think that's roughly it anyway, it's to do with empowerment, which I really don't want to go into . . .'

'So it's like when I'm in the pub and Gary calls me a cunt?'

'Bruce!'

'No, no, Lindy, it's what Gary says – not me, so it's like when Gary calls me a cunt and he really means my good friend?'

'Well, kind of, nothing to do with empowerment but yeah it's the same but er, different.'

'So, Richard, if I had a black friend it'd be all right to call him a nigger cunt?'

'Ah. No. Not really. I reckon you'd be walking on troubled water there, Bruce, I think you'd have to know him really, really well and probably be wearing protective headgear. Anyway shall we have some coffee?'

'But . . .'

'Shut up, Bruce. That's enough. Yes, Richard, make us all a coffee, please, that would be lovely. Some of us have been up since three o'clock this morning.'

'Really, Linda?'

'Yes, really.'

'I'll have mine black.'

'Will you please be quiet, Bruce!'

Richard stands. He smiles, leans forward and touches the top of my arm.

'Arf, arf,' he whispers.

I wash the breakfast things then go out for a paper. Bruno's not fussed about another walk and I don't really feel like doing too much today either, which is just as well since as per usual there's nothing for me to do. I'm tired and the old shoulder muscles ache a bit – that bloody tree was heavier than I thought.

Back home again. I make myself a coffee, roll a fag and smooth out the *Gazette* on the kitchen table.

Blimey, top of page 5!

I know that face, I definitely know that face. Damn me if it isn't Ropey Ian himself, Mr Ian Roper esq. I knew he'd gone into teaching but now it appears he's gone into the shit and right up to his armpits by the look of it.

Local Teacher Disciplined.

Oh dear, oh dear, oh dear. It appears that our Ropey Ian, in spite of all the advantages bestowed upon him during his formative years, and despite his undisputed prowess on the old clarinet, has really come unstuck. This is great.

It says here that while Ropey was cleaning out the school gerbil, Snowy, he accidently dropped the poor little sod into a big bucket of white glue. Ropey must have panicked, I suppose, watched in horror as the last inch of Snowy's tail disappeared for ever into the milky white morass, decided it was too late to save the poor little fucker, and stupidly elected to keep his gob shut.

However, two days later when Miss Keeble elected Karen Dunn, best-behaved girl in class Y4IR, to ladle glue out into plastic cups in preparation for the final glue/glitter-based assault of the festive season, the second dredge came up with one stiff gerbil and Snowy's sudden disappearance and sticky demise was no longer just Ropey's guilty secret.

Karen's been off school ever since and her mum blabbed to the paper. Ropey Ian confessed, was carpeted by the board of governors and now the *Gazette's* rodent expert has added shit to the fire by saying that Ropey could easily have saved Snowy's furry little life if only he'd had the presence of mind (AND THAT IS WHAT WE PAY OUR TEACHERS FOR) to rinse him thoroughly under the tap.

Brilliant. Absolutely brilliant.

It's a basic bathroom. Pot pedestal, pot basin, three white tiles centred behind, white rubber plug on a worn-out chain. Next to it, a cast-iron roll-top bath with plain feet painted cream, brass bomb taps, black lino floor and white ceramic pan flushed from a lead-lined wooden tank. Plain chrome chain with a turned oak pull. A wooden plaque with a wire hoop holds half a roll of Izal, same stuff as we had in the army. John Wayne's bog roll. Rough and tough and takes no shit.

Every morning since 1905 William senior, his wife Florence and little William and Walter taking turns to crouch over, grunt out a few ounces of the dead stuff, yank the chain, get rid of the dirty business then get straight back to the serious business of being the most perfect Edwardian family in town.

My favourite room in the house, this bathroom, bare and functional, not festooned with all the frills and fancies of the rest of the place.

Little treat for me today. Up at silly o'clock this a.m. all excited. Toddled off into town, came back with toothbrushes, four of – bathroom for the cleaning of – a pair of marigolds and ten tailor-mades for smoking after.

Next week they clean for a fortnight, then put the house to bed, cover the furniture, put little tissue hats on all the pottery, pathetic waste of time if you ask me, but the Trust says and Linda does.

Linda runs workshops, which is clever. My Lindy's really not half as stupid as she looks. Posh ladies pay good money to get down on their hands and knees and do half the work. They love it, the Trust attracts a type – horsey – or at least they look like horses most of them, well off, none too bright and bored shitless.

No housework for them to do, oh no, you must be kidding. They have a woman who does. A woman who does the cooking, the cleaning, the washing, the shagging of the husband, the walking the kids, the picking up of the dog from school, the whole caboodle. So for these redundant, slack-faced, toffee-arsed bitches taking two hours to clean the crud off a worthless worn-out kitchen chair using a wad of cotton waste soaked in meths is an adventure and it makes the tea and cakes which Linda sells them after taste all the better.

Anyway, next week the cleaning, conservation cleaning, begins but today Bruce Glasscock, Sergeant, retired, gives the bathroom the once-over.

First things first. I take off my shirt and fold it over the side of the bath, think about it then decide to dispense with the trousers too – no point bagging the knees of my second-best pair of elephant cords. I fold them carefully, place them on top of the shirt, line up the furrows and smooth out the seams.

I always do that before I hit the hay as well, lay out the old clothes properly, force of habit from my army days partly, I like to think the clothes are getting a good kip even if I'm not.

Next I fill a bucket. I've forgotten the bucket. I go back up into the attic of the Hays through the connecting door into our, Linda's, house. I take a square red bucket from outside Kay's store cupboard on the top landing, shake some soapflakes into it, head down the stairs to our bathroom and bump straight into Richard.

'What the hell do you think you are doing in here, young man,' I bellow at him and try to hold my stomach in.

'It's snowing out, Bruce, haven't you seen? Linda said I could use your loo, save me having to go outside in it.'

'Oh, well, that's all right then.'

'Nice pants, Bruce. Not seen that colour since the '70s.'

He nips into the bathroom. I hear him lift the seat then slash. Flushes and he comes out smiling. He looks me up and down.

'Nice gloves an' all, Bruce. Yellow rubber, ooh I say. See you later, big boy.' He grins and minces back down the stairs chuckling to himself.

Ordinarily I'd have followed him downstairs. Ordinarily I'd have followed him down to the kitchen, ordinarily I'd have torn a strip off the cocky little shit but not today, today is special and I'd better get to it.

I half-fill the bucket from the gold-plated hot tap of our avocado plastic bath and carry it back upstairs. I march across the top landing into Hays, and proceed in an orderly manner down one flight to the bathroom.

Right, ready. Ready at last.

First toothbrush is red and I like that – it matches the bucket, clashes horribly with the pants – but this is not a flaming fashion parade, Glasscock, oh no. Oh no, no, no, no, no, no. There is work to be done.

I tear the thin cellophane packing away from the toothbrush, screw it up, then take a moment to compose myself. Job to be done, soldier. All you ever wanted and all you ever need. Fuck's sake, pull yourself together, man. Snap to it, boyo, wind in yer neck, tuck in yer bollocks and shut the fuck up.

It's quiet. I feel the time going, feel it moving, feel the precious seconds slipping by. I hear the cellophane creaking, ticking away, as it struggles to get back into shape. Time to go. Get myself back, get myself back into shape. Corrupted, clueless, cunt-whipped and creaking. Rotting to fuck in this shitty, dusty, fucking shithole.

One small fucking thing. One small fucking thing, Glasscock – can you fucking manage that, soldier? Can you fucking manage that, get something fucking right for a fucking change, do something fucking properly, you fucking useless, limp-dicked, little useless little fucking cunt? One small fucking thing you can fucking get completely fucking right.

Glad and sorry. Mind like a sewer, memory like a

sieve. Time to face the music, Glasscock. Only the Green Howards never taught you how to fucking dance.

Deep breath. Start at the top and work down.

I whisk the toothbrush into the suds, then I work it around the inside edge of the first of the pair of brass hinges which hold the seat and lid together and connect the whole lot to the white ceramic pan.

You wouldn't know they were brass, these hinges, they're bright green, these chaps, but twenty minutes later hinge number one, left-hand side of the bog, Hays House, Maple Grove, Gateford, South Yorks, England, the UK, Planet Earth, shines like burnished gold.

They had a meeting about that. Can you believe they actually sat down and had a meeting about whether to clean the hinges on the bog? Well, they did. In agony they were. I know this because they had it in our kitchen and I was coffee wallah.

Do we or do we not remove the patina? Only the way Simon said it was 'pah-teen-ah'. Simon made dirt sound like a fucking curry, but Arabella the chief conservator for this region, a nice-looking lass, well stacked, good legs, nice arse, and so posh she could hardly speak, soon put our Simon straight on that one.

'Oh no, Simon,' she says, sounding like she's got the Elgin Marbles in her gob. 'I weally must interject at this junctuah. In this particulah case it can scarcely be descwibed as parteenarh. What we are dealing with he-are, the pwoblem we harve before us, is a pair of alwedy wickety hinges coated with verdigwi.'

And for a second when she said that word she actually became French. You know those dippy bints you see on the holiday programmes who say 'Pari' instead of 'Paris'? And when they say 'Pari' their faces go all pointy and foreign like they're remembering a holiday there?

Well, when Arabella said verdigwi she tossed back her head, her black tousled ringlets tumbled across her heaving shoulders, her tits got even bigger, her eyes glinted, her face went all sweaty and she actually became French, stupid cow.

So then Linda chimes in. She's been sat there all quiet, listening quietly to the world's poshest twat contest being broadcast live from her kitchen, and her face is flashing like a beetroot wired to the mains.

'They had a maid,' she says. 'William senior and his wife Florence had a maid – William and Walter kept her on after their parents died. They didn't want anything to change. That's the whole point of this place in case you've forgotten, Simon. The Hays always had a maid. Her wages are in William senior's cashbook and she's mentioned in William and Walter's diaries time and again. If she'd have let the muck build up on those hinges, the stair rods, the surround on the doormat well, the door furniture, the bib taps over the kitchen sink, the handles on the coal scuttle, the trim on the front-room fireplace, or anything else brass in this place, she'd've had her marching orders, patina or not.'

'Ah. Yes. Good point, Linda, so that will be our

policy regarding the brarse, but no abrasives if you please and just clean the hinges in the er, bathroom on an annual basis.'

'Thank you, Simon. I wouldn't have used abrasives anyway and I agree about the hinges. I do know my job. Can we get on?'

I could have kissed her, held her in my arms and kissed her on the mouth, but I never. I made some more coffee instead, served it to each of them in a dirty cup. See how they rated the patina on that.

I take my red toothbrush to the basin and turn on the tap. The tap wheezes for a few seconds then coughs out a dose of rusty water; first time it's run for twelve months. Soon as the water runs clear I stick the plug in and let the basin fill. I rinse the toothbrush and give the first hinge a good going over with fresh water. Right. Hinge Number Two. Now we're getting somewhere. By the time I've finished with this bathroom, by the time I've finished in here, worked the old Glasscock magic on the fixtures and fittings, walls, window and floor, Her Majesty the Queen could pay a visit. She could eat her dinner off the floor in here if she wanted, and after, and only if she felt like it, she could sit astride the newly polished throne, drop her regal knickers, tinkle her queenly ivories for a while. Bring herself off to a right royal climax.

I wonder sometimes if Linda does it, touches herself, tinkles her ivories, licks her own stamps.

They were all at it in the army, the ladies.

The Women's Royal Army Corps, Weekly Ration of

Army Cunt. Go into any WRAC's quarters, and check the fire-extinguishers – water-filled jobs they were – each one fitted with a WRAC's Delight. CO_2 charge cylinder about seven inches long and one in diameter. They were always missing.

'I've brought you a coffee, Bruce. You've been in here ages, and you must be freezing in just your er, pants. I'm cold and I've got me thermals on. And before you say anything, I know food and drink's not allowed but Linda said seeing as it's the bathroom a coffee'd be OK.'

'Thanks. Thanks very much, Richard.'

'Making waves in the bathroom, eh, Bruce?'

'What?'

'It's a song, Bruce, don't worry about it. I heard voices as I came in – were you talking to yourself?'

'Don't think so, might have been, I suppose.'

'Second sign of madness, Bruce, that and hairs on the palm of your hand.'

And I can't help checking and Richard can't help noticing.

'First sign is looking for 'em. Can't believe you fell for that one, mate – it's the oldest gag in the world.'

He just called me mate. No one does that.

'Do you think we can risk a fag, Bruce?'

'Blimey, don't know about that. Have you any idea how much shit we'll be in if Linda catches us?'

'She won't. She's just gone out. Taken Bruno for a walk, said she needed a break, he needed to go for a, well, he needed, and you could get on. Anyway, I have a plan. With your brains and my looks, Bruce, well, we're completely fucked, but we can lock the door, hang out the window and flush the dog-ends away after. Like we were kids. Now is that a plan or what?'

'I haven't got my baccy. It's in the kitchen.'

'It's OK, have one of mine, same stuff anyway. I should talk to you about that sometime. Do you pay full price for yours?'

'What?'

'Do you buy your baccy in the shops?'

'Yes. Yes, I do.'

'Well, don't. You must be the only person in England. Next time you need some, let me know.'

Richard hands me a green plastic pouch of Golden Virginia with the health warning on in Dutch, a packet of green Rizlas written on in French and a cylindrical Cricket lighter with Smarties printed on it. I roll a fag.

I hand the baccy back to Richard and snap the bolt to while he rolls an even thinner one than usual, then I lift the narrow sash. I spark him, then myself. We hang out of the window shoulder to shoulder, our elbows touching on the stone sill. The snow spirals through the slot between the Hays and Rebecca's house next door and clots the back lawn, three-day stubble, spiky green beard poking through flat white make-up. Saw that in a film once, don't remember which one.

'Anyway, *compadre*, how's *your* love life?'

'What?'

'You asked me, now I'm asking you. Linda seems a nice lady.'

'Yeah, she is.'

'So anyway, are Linda's tits a nice warm handful? I'll pass on the sloppy seconds too if you don't mind, you randy old goat.'

'Sometimes, sometimes I . . . I'm sorry, Richard. I'm sorry.'

'You want to watch it, mate. I'm not that bothered, in fact I'm not even going to get into this, but I know what you're up to and I'm not having it. I'll spare you the self-righteous volunteer speech, good works and all that shite. I'm here to learn the business, so this is a free course for me, but you'll come to a sticky end one day, or you'll come unstuck.

'All through school I had this, Bruce, and you know what? A year ago I found out where he lived. My mate Sean put his windows through while I dropped a pound and a half of sugar in his petrol tank. On a scale of one to ten it was the best. Like they say, don't get mad, get eleven.'

Richard smiles at his own weak little joke and touches the top of my arm with the back of his hand. He lets it fall and I realise I'm pretty much naked. I thought I could have this one, break his face if necessary – now I'm not so sure. He's got me locked in a room, trapped in a window, breaking all the rules and I'm pretty much naked.

'It always comes in threes,' Linda says, waving a form.

'What's that, Lindy?'

'It always comes in threes, first the roof, then the paper peeling off in Mother's bedroom and now there's beetle in the attic. I'll have to send a report, they'll have to come and check, they'll have to do a report and when that's been approved we'll have to completely clear out the room and store all the stuff somewhere while they get it treated. This is going to set us back weeks. Me and Kay were doing the attic yesterday, the lumber room, and you know how much stuff's up there.'

'You mean useless junk.'

'No, Bruce. I do not. Anyway, we cleared the whole lot to one side, took up the newspaper off the floor all ready for the clean and there's holes in some of the boards. Not many – but I'm sure they weren't there this time last year. I think it might be woodworm.'

'Or ants?'

'What's that, Richard?'

'Only joking. Can I have a look?'

Richard stubs out his rollie, scrapes his chair back across the kitchen floor and stands up.

'See you shortly, sensation-seekers.'

He trots down the hallway and bounds up our stairs taking the steps two at a time without asking. We hear his footsteps thump across the top landing.

'What's fucking wrong with him anyway? And since when does he use our stairs without asking?'

'Since I told him he could, Bruce. Kay does, it's quicker – saves her having to go outside and cuts down wear on the Hays stair carpet.'

'Ah yes, of course, the famous carpet. The Axminster stair carpet with an Egyptian design cost £7 9s 6d in 1923 when patterns such as this blah blah blah. How many meetings have there been about that fucking carpet? Anyway Kay works here, Richard's just a volunteer.'

'Don't swear, Bruce. Richard works here too now. Just because we, the Trust, don't pay doesn't mean it's not work. I think he's lonely, his girlfriend's away in Scotland on a course. He just gets a bit giddy sometimes. He likes it here.

'I'm very pleased with Richard, actually. We've got through more work in the three months he's been here than we did in the last six. He's keen, he's careful, he's great with the visitors and Kay really likes him.'

'Hey there, Linda, don't have a cow.'

'Sorry, Richard?'

'Nothing, Linda. I'm starting to wonder if you ever watch television – all these top cultural references going up in smoke.'

'What?'

142

'Nothing, honestly, and thanks for the big up. I'll definitely be asking you for a reference. I am a bit lonely actually – you know when you find yourself talking just that little bit too much to people down the shops? And yes I do like it here.'

'You heard what I just said?'

'Oh yeah,' he says, 'and it's all true and I am fantastic; lonely saviour of the Hays House at your service. Don't know how you ever managed without me here, Linda.'

Linda smiles and her neck goes pink.

'So did you see the holes?'

'Yeah, Linda, I sure did, lady. I checked 'em out all right and I'm here to tell ya, missy, them are bitching holes.'

Lindy looks at me with a big cartoon question mark branded into her forehead and I know this is the time. Big chance to say something. Scythe the little cunt off at the knees, cut him down to size. The wisdom of age and experience triumphs over youth and exuberance. But I can't. Richard's alive and he's full of it. I can't think of a single fucking thing.

'How old are you, Richard?'

'I'm twenty-nine actually, Bruce, but I've kept my looks and I am still cool with the kids.'

'What kids?'

'It's just an expression, Bruce. I'm being ironically postmodern this morning and I'm only mucking about.'

'What?'

'I'm joking, Bruce, but things sure have changed up here on Waltons Mountain.'

'What, what the fuck are you on about?'

'Bruce, I've told you . . .'

'Sorry, Linda.'

'Anyway,' he says, 'like I said, don't have a . . . don't worry. It's definitely woodworm, about twenty holes, not sure if it's active even. Take ten minutes tops to treat it.'

I can feel myself brewing up. That little cunt. Linda's little miracle.

'So you think you can deal with this, do you, Richard, same as that ridiculous nonsense about the roof?'

'Yep, you can buy little cans of Cuprinol, about three pounds they are, like an aerosol but with a pointy nozzle on the end. You stick that in the holes, give it a quick squirt and for you, Herr Voodwerm, zee war is over.'

'Is that it?' Linda asks. 'Is that all you do?'

'Yeah, and I bet that's all the Trust'd do. But from what you said about the roof it'd cost a lot more than three of your Earth pounds. If you're worried we'll count the holes, put a little pencil ring round each one we treat and check in a couple of weeks. If there's any more we'll treat 'em again, or you could report it then.'

'But they'd know we knew about it before. How'd we explain that?'

'Ah ha, Linda,' he says, tapping the side of his head with his thumb, 'not only am I good-looking, I am also clever, modest and there's mathod in my medness. That's why I said pencil, baby, just rub it out and act surprised. Now is that a plan or what?'

He called her baby. The little cunt. He called my Lindy baby.

'Are you suggesting that we lie, deliberately deceive . . .'

'Shutup, Bruce. OK then, thanks, Richard. That's what we'll do. This Cuprinol stuff, where do you get it?'

'Any DIY place'll sell it.'

'Give him the keys, Bruce – no, in fact you'd better unlock the garage for us. I'll come with you, Richard, I fancy a trip out. We can stop at that new place Kay's always on about on the way back. Tea and cakes. My treat. I reckon you've just saved me about two hundred pounds and three months' upset. You can drive if you like.'

'Cool,' he says, 'Kool and the Gang.'

'What?'

'Oh Lord,' he says, 'Hays is filmed before a dead studio audience. Are you familiar with the work of Quentin Tarantino? Linda? Bruce?'

I fetch the garage key off the back of the cellar door and step outside. The snow's melted and it's raining hard.

Linda bundles into the kitchen and plonks two carriers down on the table.

'Richard's staying for tea, Bruce. He's just putting the car away. We've had a lovely time. I've got some nice steak and I bought us a bottle of wine. I've got something to tell you.'

She looks so cheerful some of it rubs off on me.

'You're in love?'

'What?'

'You're expecting?'

'No, don't be silly, Bruce.'

'What then?'

'I've offered Richard the house.'

'Whadyamean, you can't just give it away, it's not even yours to give and anyway, where would we live?'

'No, the House. The Hays House after I leave.'

'We're leaving?'

'Bruce, do you ever listen to a single word I say?'

'What's that, dear?'

'Oh very funny, you can peel the spuds for that, soldier. Don't you remember the morning Gary brought the ladder round so Richard could mend the roof?'

'Gary brought a ladder round? Richard mended the roof?'

'Blimey, Bruce. I knew I never should have married you. I should've just got a rabbit or something.'

'A rabbit?'

'Yes, Bruce, a rabbit. Do you really not remember any of this?'

'No, not really, dear.'

'Well, the same day Gary brought the ladder round I had a phone call from Simon.'

'Ah well, that jumped-up little shit.'

'Bruce, let me finish. He said there was a custodian's job coming up at Lightwick Manor.'

'Limpwick Manor? Sounds like my kinda place.'

'Lightwick Manor. It's a great big place, it's got a full-time staff, a restaurant, they even film period dramas there sometimes. It'd be better money and we'd get our own little house on the estate, so you wouldn't need to have anything to do with the volunteers or the other staff.'

'He said that? Why would he say that?'

'You know full well why he said that – it's no use pretending what's happened before's never happened – and that way we'd have more privacy too.'

'I'd still get you back in the evenings, Lindy? Have you all to myself at the end of each day?'

'Oh Bruce, of course you will, darling, you can be so sweet sometimes. There'd be things happening in the evenings now and again, just like there are here, but mostly, yes, we'd still have our evenings together. It'd

148

be like a new start for us. Anyway, do you want to get the spuds on?'

'Hold on, you've not told me about Richard, and when are we leaving?'

'No, no, that's right. So I said to Simon, I said to him that I didn't want to leave the Hays straightaway 'cause we've not finished all the cataloguing, at least not until the end of next season, and he said that was fine as the new job wouldn't be available till then anyway, and so I mentioned how pleased I was with Richard, and asked if I trained him up would Simon consider him as the new custodian of the Hays?'

'So it's not definite?'

'What's not definite?'

'Richard. That Richard's getting this place?'

'No, it's not definite. You know the Trust, nothing ever is, but if Richard's got a year's experience – what do they call it? hands on – and a good reference from me, he should get it. This isn't your typical Trust property – a lot of the people who're after a stately home wouldn't look twice at this place, or they'd just look down on it, too much like hard work – and most of the other candidates wouldn't have the right experience. They'll have to advertise it, obviously, but Richard should walk it if he cuts out the silly comments.'

'I thought you liked his silly comments.'

'I do, but it doesn't do to play the fool in front of those people – you know how seriously they take themselves. I told Richard as much this afternoon.'

'So what did he say?'

'Well, this is the funny thing, Bruce, the reason why I think I've done the right thing, why I feel so cheerful now. He cried, he just broke down and cried, right in the middle of the tearooms.'

'So he said yes?'

'Yes, course he said yes. He was so chuffed. He said he couldn't wait to tell his girlfriend. There is one thing though.'

'There always is, there's always a catch. Always. What? No, don't tell me, he's been in prison.'

'Why d'you say that, Bruce?'

I must say how I'm enjoying this little chat. Lindy asking me questions, listening to my answers even, her face glowing in the twilight, and I fall in love again just like back then.

'Have you seen how the little shit rolls his fags? Have you seen them? Like matchsticks they are. I bet he's got tattoos as well.'

'Bruce, I wish you wouldn't talk about him like that. Anyway you've got army tattoos, and not very nice ones either. He's very fond of you, you know, he told me about the books he got you, the poetry.'

'The what? What's he been saying about me, behind my back?'

'The First World War poetry and the Lyn Mac-donald books.'

'Oh them. I forgot. Anyway, so what's wrong with him?'

'There's nothing wrong with him. You're right though, Bruce, he does have a tattoo, it's nice, a sun at the top of his arm. I saw it when we were shifting the piano in the back parlour. But there's nothing wrong with him, at least I don't think there is.'

'So what's this one thing? This famous one thing?'

'Richard asked me, when he'd stopped crying, he asked me if it mattered that he had a criminal record.'

Back door rattles and Richard comes in. Linda flashes me a talk-about-it-later look.

'It's snowing again,' Richard says. 'Like a barsteward actually. Not too sure how I feel about all that wet white stuff dropping on the roof of me and Clare's future pomme de terre.'

'Don't start, Richard,' Linda snaps, but she's smiling. 'And never speak French in front of Bruce either. It sends him wappy.'

'OK,' he says. 'OK, Linda, I won't.'

Slept with Linda. Not *Slept*. Not like that, didn't have carnival knowledge or anything. But we did share a bed. I've Richard to thank for that.

I like my evenings with Lindy, look forward to them. We have the telly on but we don't really watch it, Linda does her needlepoint, I have my book and we sit together. Linda's off duty and she stops bossing me. Well, to a certain extent.

Anyway, not last night. We had tea, nice drop of wine, Lindy even got the candles out. Snow falling outside, kitchen lovely and warm from the Aga, Bruno curled up asleep in front of it and the three of us chatting away like lifelong friends. Like some fucking unreal outake from an Andy Williams Christmas Special it was, but it was still nice.

Rebecca popped in later, caught us drinking wine.

'I've caught you now,' she said, 'I've caught you drinking wine,' and then she fetched a bottle from next door. Brought a little visitor with her, a little terrier. Bit of companionship for her since her stupid bastard of a husband flitted with Little Miss Windowlicker, so she says.

Alfie his name is, and he's super. Alfie trots over and paws at Bruno's face. Bruno wakes, nuzzles Alfie and starts licking him, just like that. They're friends now. They sit together in front of the Aga, two little friends pretty as a picture. Linda takes a picture, and I tell my talking frog joke. Everybody laughs, especially me.

It's late and it's still snowing. Linda says why don't you stay over, Richard, you can have Bruce's room, and I'm thinking uh oh, sofa for me tonight.

I go out with Richard, take Bruno for a spin round the block and Richard takes Alfie. Last knockings they call it round here.

We walk the new friends round the block and I tell Richard all about Stony. He laughs so hard he has to grab my arm to keep him from falling down in the snow. It's clean and white, except for the patch the new friends just used, and Richard says something about not eating yellow snow. I can tell from the tone of his voice it's a joke. I don't understand but I laugh a bit just to be polite.

'You didn't understand that really,' he says. 'You just laughed a bit to be polite.'

I say that I didn't and I did. He says something about Frank. Frank Zappa.

'It's a song,' he says. 'It's famous.'

I ask him what the fuck kind of name is Zappa.

'He's dead,' Richard says. 'Cancer. And if you think Zappa's a daft name you want to check out the kids. Moon Unit and Dweezil.'

I ask him how he knows all this stuff.

'I just do,' he says.

We come back to hot cocoa, we come back to two flushed and radiant women, we come back to warm towels for the dogs. Rebecca leaves and Richard goes to bed. Linda touches my shoulder and goes upstairs. I lock up. I make myself a coffee, roll a fag and sit in the kitchen. I'm happy, Linda's happy, Richard's happy, Bruno's happy and the way things are tonight, I suspect even Moon and Dweezil might have cheered up a bit, come to terms with their ridiculous names and Frank's unfortunate demise.

I smoke the fag, and as I sit there I think I'll probably never be this happy again. And that makes me really sad. I tidy up the kitchen and put the alarm on. 1866, easy enough code to remember, last time we kicked the Krauts minus one hundred years, last time we got fucked by the Frogs plus eight hundred.

I go into the upstairs sitting room and there's nothing – the fat cow's not even closed the curtains and it's freezing in there. I poke my head round Linda's door and ask her where the blankets are.

'Not tonight, soldier,' she squeaks from under the covers. 'It's cold. You're in here with me.'

I don't know what to do. I approach the bed and slip my hand under the covers, I run it across her front, then down, and she's naked, well almost. My palm snags up around her waist. She's retained the pants. I strip off and do the same. I slip under the covers and Lindy turns her back. We lie like spoons, her soft round arse against my stomach, me cradling her breasts and not even a flicker from down below.

It's warm, I'm soft and she smells lovely. I cry myself to sleep.

There's a knock on the door and Richard steps in. 'Morning, lovebirds,' he says, 'sleep well?' He sets a tea tray down on the bedside table.

Linda starts squawking, making the kind of confused chicken noises all women produce when they're flustered.

'Richard,' she snaps, 'Richard, would you mind, would you mind very much not just waltzing in here?'

'Oh, I'm sorry,' he says, 'just thought you might fancy a spot of room service. Kay's downstairs, it's ten, and it says in the diary you're due at Clumber by eleven.'

Linda's making chicken noises now, so high-pitched that only dogs can hear them.

'Right,' says Richard. 'I'll leave you to it.'

He's hardly out the door before Linda's in her dressing gown, pulling out drawers at random and cursing. Effing and blinding she is, proper army stuff I've not heard her do in a long time, and it dawns on me this is the first morning for over three years we've woken in the same bed.

I wonder if she's like this every morning. A whole part of her day I know nothing about, her crashing around, swearing like a trooper, getting it out of her system before she emerges all calm and businesslike, ready to face the day.

I love to watch a woman dress. It's all the sweeter if you've just had them, but you can't have everything. Linda selects a bra from the top left-hand drawer of her pine chest, a big white lacy number I didn't even know she had, then turns her back and lets the dressing gown fall away.

Christ, I nearly missed it. If there's a world record for applying a bra, I'm pretty damn sure my Lindy just broke it. Straps over shoulders, wriggle the necessary into cups, pincer movement round the back, clip the clasp and it's over. She slides on a pair of dark-blue cotton trousers and plucks a cream silk blouse from the closet. It's her best one, the one with shoulder pads, appliqué collar and cuffs – so it must be an important meeting she's got this morning. Linda turns and buttons the blouse in her dressing-table mirror. She latches the buttons from the top and smooths the blouse down over her breasts. She looks lovely, and if you know it's there, you can still make out the faint outline of the brassière under the soft cream fabric.

'You look lovely, Linda. Important, is it? Important meeting this morning?'

'You still here, Bruce? Planning on lying around in bed all morning, are we, soldier? Why don't you try something useful and make some tea, you good-for-nothing, backsliding squaddie.'

You know that moment, you're relaxing in a hot

bath, maybe a shot of Radox for good measure. You feel warm, you feel safe and just for a moment everything's perfect in your sad little world. Then the cold tap decides to drop its guts all over your fucking foot.

I feel like I've just been slapped, but I quite like it.

I pull my clothes on doublequicktime, get the tray and I'm halfway out the door. Linda finishes pinning her cameo brooch, then pins my elbow between her thumb and forefinger.

'Tell anyone about this, soldier, and your feet won't touch.'

'Of course, Lindy, I mean no. I won't.'

She's smiling though.

Downstairs it's still like the Waltons. Rebecca's here with Alfie, Bruno's in doggie heaven, Kay's sat at the table with Richard. They're talking about trains for some reason.

I stick the kettle on, open the back door and crunch out into the snow. Bright sunshine and a clear blue sky. A perfect picture postcard of a day – all we need now is for fucking Heidi to pop round, borrow a cup of sugar, burst into song.

I take two crisp lungfuls of clean white air then go back into the kitchen.

'So what's this about a criminal record then, Richard? Been a bad lad, have we, drugs was it, or maybe a spot of interfering with the kiddies?'

Kay's up and out, Rebecca's standing to leave. Then Linda comes down.

'What's going on, Bruce?'

'Oh nothing, Linda, nothing really, just asking our little criminal here a few direct questions to which I will be requiring a few direct answers before I telephone the police. Think we'd better find out exactly what this young man's been up to. He stayed in our house last night, remember, our home, he could have taken anything. Empty your pockets, you little bastard. Now.'

Richard stands.

'OK, Bruce,' he says, 'I will.'

'Oh no, please, Richard,' Linda says. 'There's really no need for that, really.'

I can feel it, feel the sap rising. On top of the situation, Glasscock, stay on top. Take control, make the little bastard sweat. Tear him off a strip then shit on him from a great height.

'This is my house and I say what goes. When I say jump, you jump, my fine young fellow. Now empty your fucking pockets or I'll do it for you.'

'Be quiet, Bruce,' Linda snaps. 'That's enough. It's not your house, it's my house. Have you taken your pills this morning?'

'No, er, no, I was just going to.'

'Well, you just do that, Bruce, do it now and calm down. I'll make us all some tea and we can settle this once and for all.'

She clicks the kettle on. It rumbles and clicks off straightaway. Well, it would, wouldn't it? I just boiled the fucker. Linda sets three mugs on the kitchen table and Richard rolls himself a fag, the baggiest misshapen piece of shit I've ever seen. His hands are shaking.

'Right,' he says. 'When I was a student you were allowed to sign on during the summer holidays. You can't now, but back in the early '80s you could. You also got your rent paid, housing benefit they call it, well, you can't do that either now, not students anyway. So, at the start of the summer holidays I signed on, we all did, filled in the housing-benefit forms and stuff, and after a few weeks it started getting paid. At the end of the hols we all signed off again but by mistake they kept on sending me the housing cheques and I kept on paying them in. I think their departments were supposed to talk to each other but they never.'

'Is that it?'

'Yeah, Linda, that's it.'

'How long for?'

'Well, for nearly a year actually. It's no excuse but I was skint. Anyway, they caught up with me, made an example of me. I reckon I wasn't the only one, but that's by the by, and I got done for fraud. I just thought you should know. Anyway it's lapsed now, but I still thought it was best if you knew now rather than it coming out later on, if the Trust did a police check or something.'

'So you went to court?'

'Oh yeah, I went to court all right. Like I say, they made an example of me, saw it as a misuse of my education, I think that's the phrase they used, said it was a very clever fraud, which it wasn't at all. I just kept on paying the cheques into my bank. If anything it was a very stupid fraud.'

'So what happened?'

'I got community service, sixty hours they gave me, painting and decorating mostly. I quite enjoyed it actually, and I met some right likely lads, then the council made me pay the money back, bit at a time.'

'Did you hear that, Bruce?'

'Yes, yes I did. He's still a criminal though. Under our roof. He should have told us the first day, put it on his world-famous CV.'

'Don't be stupid, Bruce. You don't put things like that on a CV. Why didn't you tell us before though, Richard?'

'It never came up. Not till yesterday when you offered me, said there was a chance I might get the Hays and said about a reference. That's why I told you when I did. Anyway, is it really a problem? I mean, I'm not proud of it obviously, but it's not exactly crime of the century, is it?'

Well, I like that. One minute he's confessing, telling us he's a common criminal, a fraudster if you please, and the next he's all cocky making jokes. If any son of mine, if he ever did anything like that, well, I don't know what I'd do. Lindy's with me on this one, I can feel it.

I clear my throat all ready for the big one. This is it, the last big push, the end of a perfect twenty-four hours, the magic moment when I chuck the little cunt out in the snow, slam the door and show Linda once and for all who wears the fucking trousers round here.

Think I'll stand up for this bit. I stand up, scrape the chair back across the floor, as much noise as possible required here for maximum dramatic effect. I clear my throat again.

'Ahem, ahg ag ag . . .'

'No, Richard,' Linda pipes up all chirpy. 'No, of course it's not a problem, specially if it's already lapsed. I'm just glad it's nothing serious.'

'Nothing serious, woman, nothing serious? Have you gone fucking mad? Nothing serious!'

'Get out, Bruce, and take Bruno with you. Out.'

She chucks me out in the snow then slams the door behind me.

Linda pays me seventeen pounds a week – an insult at my time of life. I get my army pension, not the full whack as I'm a brown-letter man – I came out early on account of the old nerves. I'm supposed to be saving that, putting it by for when Linda retires so we can get ourselves a little place somewhere, make it bright, make it neat, then die. Then there's always the odd pound here and there from petty cash. If she sends me out I keep the change. She never notices, or if she does she's never said anything.

It's bloody cold out here and I convince myself I can afford it. Ten minutes later I press the button on the gunshop, the frame buzzes and I'm in. They've a sale on.

Frank stubs his panatella in the ashtray, the upturned top of a Landy piston I gave him years ago. Frank mentions to me about the sale. A pre-Christmas half-price event he calls it. He collects stuff like that does Frank, makes it his own then makes himself laugh.

Frank did his bathroom up last Christmas, got himself a shower with a curtain-entry system.

Frank makes me a coffee, adds a finger of Scotch without asking and lights up a fresh panatella.

'Go on,' he says. 'You know you want to.'

I try it on. Then I pay.

After that I pop into the RegNancy. There's posters everywhere and they've got the Christmas decorations up. Nancy's built a tiny stage at the far end of the lounge, crates, garden trellis, streamers, fairy lights, tinsel.

I sip my Scotch and pick a leaflet up off the bar.

Drink & Be Merry
RegNancy Hotel
Entertainments for the Festive Season

'Front Ear. What the hell's that?'

'It's a turn,' says Reg, 'a vocal group. Comedy. You know – like in *Star Trek*.'

'Penelope's Pitstop?'

'Talented hit group, only a few tickets remaining,' says Reg.

'Blendin' Jude?'

'Elvis impersonator. Half-price offers on selected beers and lagers,' says Reg.

'D' Lishus?'

'Modern female trio. Singles night. Big-screen Sky Sports,' says Reg.

'Jeff Leppard and Ian Maiden?'

'Rock disco,' says Reg.

'The Jimmy Echo Show and Quiz?'

'Hits from the '60s. Boxing Day special.'

'With a quiz after?'

'Correct, Bruce,' says Reg.

'Kids With Cancer? No, don't tell me, Reg, I'm getting the hang of this, it's one of those Gothics, those awful hard-metal groups?'

'No, Bruce, it's a charity night for kids with cancer. You coming?'

Linda's back when I get home.

'Nice jacket, Bruce – where've you had that from?'

'Oh this, oh nowhere, it's from that charity place at the end of the precinct. Cancer Research I think it is.'

'I didn't know we had one of those. We've a Sue Ryder, you know, where Kay got that carpet, and an Age Concern, but not a cancer one. Where is it exactly?'

And I'm wishing I'd done my research a bit more carefully now. Best part of two hundred spondulicks this jacket was, half-price event or not. I should have mucked it up a bit like I usually do. I shouldn't have bought it.

'So how much did you pay for that?'

'Oh I don't remember – fifty pence, I think. I got it last week, filthy it was, so I had it dry-cleaned. I've only just picked it up. I was cold.'

'Yes, well, you've only yourself to thank. Teach you to talk to Richard like that. Anyway, let's have a look. That's what they call a Norfolk jacket, isn't it? It's ever so smart. What's that on the sleeve?

Tell you what that is on the sleeve. Me caught out, me in the shit again, me not having a single moment's time to do what I want, me creeping about like an undercover cunt, me having to explain every last bloody thing to a bossy silly bloated woman. Two hundred fine English pounds it says on there. Two hundred fucking quid in clear black computer type.

'It must be the laundry tag,' I say, and peel the label off another lie.

Don't really see Lindy for the next couple of weeks.

She's tired or she's cross or both. So I keep my head down. Wind in my neck, tuck the old scrotal back into my body. Coffee, fags, coffee, fags, Bruno, shit-bags, coffee, fags, coffee, supper, bed.

She's with Richard at Clumber for the Victorian Christmas Fayre, next door with Richard for the workshops, or shut in the office with Richard chattering about the Friends' Christmas Meal.

He's here early and he stays late. Instead of the Hays or the Trust, he now says we. He's had his hair cut again.

We missed Speed Limit, we missed Whiplash, we missed Tramp & Swank, we missed The Crayzee World of Kim Le Mar and we missed Blendin' Jude at the RegNancy. Richard said he'd go to that, said Elvis impersonators always made him cry, them and brass bands. So that sounded like a laugh.

Lindy said we'd definitely go to that one. We'll definitely go, we'll all go, she said. Go with Kay and Gary. We'll get there early, sit at the front, drink selected beers and lagers at special-offer prices, relax and let our hair down.

Well, that's what she said, but we never.

Woke up this morning and thought I felt it stirring. Not stiff – no such luck – but the first twinges. That lovely feeling. The muscles tightening round the base, and the chance, the glorious possibility, that the old cock might crow again. No fucking chance. Not had a proper one in three years, excepting the photocopier-induced chub which got me in so much bother.

Convoy cock we called that in the army, the motion of a truck rubbing you to a frenzy inside the old battledress. I used to get them regular as clockwork, truck or no truck, regular as clockwork they were, cockwork even. God knows, I used to. It was up before me every morning, pumped-up and ready to perform.

Better leave your lights on, ladies, there's a monster in my bed. I used to think he was sleeping, but of late, ladies, I'm quite seriously concerned. I think the fucker might be dead.

The good old days, eh?

Married quarters for me and Lindy, and, if just a shag at daybreak was out of the question, an early-morning hand-shandy refreshed the parts special offers on selected beers and lagers could never reach, and I'd meet the day with a song in my heart, filth in my head and power in my blood.

I can't even do that any more, I've tried. I picture Lindy spread, I picture her folded over a chair, I picture Lindy the human wheelbarrow, frilly panties pulled aside, tits bouncing with every thrust, but there's nothing.

I loved it when I was a lad. Wednesdays I'd get home from school early, half day on account of it being a posh school, let myself in, take off my maroon uniform jacket, fetch a bit of kitchen roll from the kitchen, or a bit of toilet roll from the toilet, or a paper serviette from the sideboard if Dad had a new film in.

Half a foolscap page of narrow feint and a list of titles in biro, ticks by his favourites.

MISDEMEANOURS AT BIG BOOB MANOR.

My very own very favourite, and, looking at the number of ticks by it, Dad's as well. Hidden in a cutlery box, the one the firm gave Grandad when he retired.

There was a lock on it but I found the key.

Inside, a stack of thin blue boxes, and inside each one of them a plastic reel loaded with a spiral of super 8 shot in Holiday Colour with a soundstripe down the left-hand edge.

I drag the projector out from behind the sofa and unlatch the gold metal clasps on the red-and-grey rexine case. The grey lid comes away and leaves the projector mounted on a red plinth which has the amplifier and speaker inside it. I lift the projector on to the tile-topped coffee table my dad made at evening class, plug in and slip the full reel of film on to the rear capstan. I snap over the catch which holds it, feed the leader into the gate, switch on for a second as the film spews through, switch off, then wind the leader on to the empty front spool. I close the curtains and move Mum's cheeseplants to one side – which gives me a screen of bare white wall.

I settle on the rug, tuck my legs under the coffee table, prop my back against the base of the sofa and undo my maroon uniform trousers. I ease my right hand into my pants and under my freshly dropped bollocks and click the forward switch with my left. There's a burst of scratchy white light and the smell of ironing as the dust burns away.

The film opens with an extended shot of horses fucking.

It's the day before the day before Christmas Eve. Christmas Eve, eve, eve. And today we have a social event, *the* Social Event of the Hays calendar. The Friends of the Hays House Christmas Lunch, a thank you to the Friends for all their work over the past year and clever Lindy's way of making sure they'll help us next.

Linda's had her hair done, Bruno's had a bath and I'm instructed to wear my new Norfolk jacket on the strict understanding that I tell no one it's from a charity shop – which makes me smile at any rate.

Richard lets himself in the back door without knocking, says hello and makes a fuss of Bruno.

'Don't you look smart, boy?' he says. 'Is that a new collar?'

'It is,' says Linda. 'Bruce's bathed him too, and don't you look smart, Richard? Is that a new suit?'

'No,' he says. 'I've had it ages but I went mad and got it cleaned. Last time I wore this suit, blimey, last time I wore this suit I was in court and it got a bit, er, sweaty.'

Linda ignores that.

'Do you cook, Richard?'

'No,' he says. 'I've tried, but it always turns out orange.'

'Well, you'd better learn – it's an important part of being custodian here. Bruce, you'd best get that fire lit. They'll all be here in an hour and it's still freezing in there.'

The kitchen fills with women. Rebecca comes in brandishing a platter of mince pies covered in cling film followed by Kay carting enough cheese to fuel a million nightmares. The babbling begins.

Richard makes eye contact. He looks uncomfortable, panicky, out of place in here this morning, even for the college-boy ponce he is, and for once I take pity on the little cunt.

'Come with me, Richard,' I say. 'You might learn something.'

I pick up yesterday's paper and go through to the exhibition room – what would be our front parlour if we had the whole house instead of having to live upstairs like a pair of fucking squirrels.

I open the door to the exhibition room. It's my fourth Christmas here and it still catches me. They've transformed it. A long table, soft white cloth, gleaming place settings, glowing table dressings, swags and tails around the fireplace and a tree all done in white and silver. It looks dandy – she is clever, my Linda, she really is clever. All it needs now is a roaring fire.

Linda's right though, it's bloody freezing in there. There's a pair of electric radiators under the window but nobody's thought to plug them in.

I plug them both in. I spread newspaper on the hearth to save the trousers from smuts, then upend the entire coalbox into the fireplace. It should be dry at any rate, the coals have been sat here gathering dust for a whole year, strictly for decorative purposes only, but today they're going to burn. Any last requests, fellas?

Just inside the chimney and just out of sight of the visitors there's a poker, my secret weapon. Big chance here to show our Mr Smartarse here something, cut him back to scale a little. Richard pokes his head into the fireplace and I stand over him holding the poker.

'Aren't you going to use anything, Bruce? Twisted-up bits of paper, kindling, all that stuff. I used to watch my gran do this when I was a kid. She had it off to a fine art.'

'Am I fuck. Watch this.'

I unfurl three feet of spiralled metal tube from around the shank of my secret weapon. To the left of the fireplace, where the high skirting joins the marble surround, is a round brass plate bolted to the woodwork. It hinges up and underneath it is a nozzle. I plug the bayonet fitting on the end of the tube into the nozzle. Gas begins fizzing out of the poker. I spark it up with my Zippo and ram a hot jet of cold blue flame right into the heart of the mound of coals.

After a cushy twelve-month posting of ornamental duties, those idle cunts probably thought they'd got away with it. A whole year of swinging the lead. And now this.

There's a flash as the dust burns off then the coals begin to fizzle. Save me, boss, save me, cries the biggest. No fucking chance. Burn, you black bastard. Burn.

I take a full bottle of sherry off the table, open it, pour us a glass each and roll myself a fag.

'Cheers. You smoking in here, Bruce?'

'Oh yes. Those women, Richard, those silly women, have got their arses in their hands and they will have all morning. Best thing we can do is lie doggo. You and me, young man, can do what we want till dinner, whatever the fuck we want.'

The coals are catching now so I withdraw the poker, unplug it and tuck it out of sight behind the tree.

'You know William and Walter fought in the First World War, Bruce?'

'Course I do, but I don't think they saw much action. Did much fighting. Probably why they both came back.'

We pull two chairs up in front of the fireplace, sip the sherry and smoke. Richard tells me what he's been finding out now the season's over. About how he's been going through the diaries and all the paperwork and that he's discovered that William and Walter were in the same regiment as his grandad – the Leicestershires.

He tells me about his gran, the same one who had firestarting off to such a fine art, how when he came home on leave, she had to soak her husband's uniform overnight in the garden water butt to drown the lice.

'So what happened to him?'

'He was gassed,' Richard says. 'Not properly – he took his mask off too early – it wasn't his fault. They'd sounded the all-clear – the cloud had gone – but there was still gas in his trench. They sent him back along the line to a dressing station and on the way he took a sliver of shrapnel to the face. When he reached the dressing station they left it there. It had gone in clean and they were busy. When he got back to Blighty, with metal in his face and his lungs in tatters, his brass buttons had turned green from the gas – but it had killed all the lice. Every cloud as they say.'

For a civvy Richard knows his stuff, seems to have a real idea of that war and what it was like for those poor sods. I refill our glasses.

Richard tells me how his grandad always acted funny on fireworks night, six days before the armistice and the sky full of hilarious fire, how he sat on his own with a bottle of Scotch, his annual packet of fags and his service medals – the same standard set William and Walter came away with. Richard's grandad accidentally cut off two fingers when he was seventy, using a circular saw to make kindling for the fireplace. He said nothing to his wife, just wrapped the fingers in a scarf, got into his Morris and drove himself to outpatients.

'Sounds like a nice old boy, your grandad.'

'He was, Bruce, I hardly knew him, he used to chase me round his allotment and cough a lot. I was only small when he died and I wish I'd had the chance to talk to him properly, and do you know about a week before he went his body rejected that piece of shrapnel – it came out through the roof of his mouth. He used to beat my grandma though.'

I top us up again, then again. We've an hour yet till the guests turn up, a whole hour at least.

The doorbell goes and surprise, surprise it's Councillor Stevens and his lady wife, Mrs Councillor Stevens. They like a drink, those two, always the first to arrive and the last to leave. He's not a bright man, our councillor, and he's very impressed that he is a councillor. Lindy says he's a self-made man who got the drawing upside-down, but his heart's in the right place and I like him well enough.

Last year we had a meeting to discuss extending the greenhouse or something, and I think it would be safe to say that Councillor Stevens had had a few too many over lunch and that there was probably something else on his mind. He was chairing the meeting for the Friends – it was only in the Hays exhibition room but Stevens blusters in like he's entering the council chamber . . .

'There's bin allegations flying about,' he thunders. 'Allegations about mis, misaprop, about me spendin' money that I shouldn't 'ave. Now will the alligator please stand up.' Councillor Stevens sat down and promptly fell asleep. After a short embarrassed silence Linda phoned him a taxi.

Richard takes Councillor and Mrs Stevens' coats and ushers them into the exhibition room. I pour them a sherry and another one for myself. The doorbell's going every five minutes and the room's filling up now, the great and the good, head of the local Chamber of Commerce and her husband, the Editor of the *Gazette* and his wife, the Vicar, assorted members of the Townswomen's Guild and mercifully nobody at all from the Trust.

Linda pokes her head round the door.

'Is everybody here?'

A big yes from all concerned.

'Right, dinner will be served in ten minutes. Could you show people to their places, Bruce, Richard.'

'Find your own,' I say. 'They're all labelled, you can all read. Yours is over here, Councillor.'

Everybody laughs and finds their own seats.

'It's right warm in 'ere,' says Councillor Stevens. 'Does anybody mind if ah cloth off?'

The Vicar looks blank even if he is a man of the cloth. The Editor of the *Gazette* and his wife look even blanker. Councillor Stevens removes his jacket anyway and loosens his tie, all the other blokes follow suit.

He picks up the sherry bottle.

'It's dead this 'un, Bruce, any chance of a refill?'

I go to the kitchen for another, fetch two from the cellarhead and head back. Linda grabs my arm.

'What did you have to go and say that for, Bruce, about them finding their own places?'

'Relax, Lindy, it was a joke. Everybody laughed, you should see it in there. We're having a great time.'

'Well, don't get carried away, Bruce, that's all.'

I uncork both bottles, hand one to Richard and we

circulate, fill everybody's glass. Crackers are popped and a rash of paper crowns breaks out around the table. There's two places spare which is odd, there should only be one.

Usually Linda sits in and me and Kay act as waiters, then eat our dinner in the kitchen. I fill a glass and take it through to Lindy.

'There's someone missing, Lindy, there's two spare seats.'

'Oh no there's not. Richard's serving with Kay this year, you're sat next to me, soldier, so watch it.' Lindy smiles and I feel like kissing her.

'Tell Richard to get in here and I'll see you in a minute.'

I take my place at the head of the table and pour myself a sherry.

'Bin promoted, 'ave you, Bruce?'

Laughter.

'No, not really, Councillor, put out to grass more like.'

More laughter.

'This young man's Richard – some of you will have met him already. He's the new long-term volunteer and we're all very pleased with the way he's fitted in. He's helping Kay serve this Christmas. By the way, Richard, boss wants you in the kitchen ASAP and I'm to behave myself.'

Richard hunches his shoulders and drags himself towards the door.

'It's a dog's life I lead and not just at Christmas,' he

groans. 'You behave yourself? How likely is that, Bruce?'

Everybody laughs again.

Linda makes a short speech.

She thanks the Friends for all their help this year, outlines next year's plans and announces the success of the Victorian Christmas Fayre.

'A certain young man,' she says, 'sold more raffle tickets this year than in the last three years put together. That might have had something to do with the fact that he told everyone first prize was the brand-new BMW parked outside in the car park when actually first prize was one of Rebecca's cakes, but we've forgiven him for that now, haven't we, Richard?'

Richard looks up from the end of the table where he's refilling wine glasses for Councillor and Mrs Stevens. He blushes.

'Did tha really do that, lad?'

'I did,' he says, 'but I had my fingers crossed behind my back – so that doesn't actually count, does it?'

'Mebbe so, mebbe not. So 'ose car were it then?'

'It was yours, Councillor.'

Sometimes you get quiet, and sometimes silence. This time there's silence and it ain't golden. Richard's face goes white and the room ices over.

'Bugger,' Councillor Stevens stage-whispers to Mrs Councillor Stevens. 'Ah bought six fuckin' books.'

It's a good two minutes before anyone's in a fit state to eat anything and when Linda stands and proposes a toast to the Hays she's still got the giggles. We drink a toast in wine to William and Walter who wasted their lives, never touched a drop and made it all possible.

Kay and Richard bring in the starters. Prawn cocktail and it's lovely. Linda's trying to have two conversations at once – one with the Vicar and his wife and another with the couple from the *Gazette* – but from time to time she turns to me, smiles, or says something to make me feel included.

I feel part of this. All the years I was stuck in the kitchen with Kay trying not to stare down her pinny, and hoping we were eating quicker than everybody else, so we wouldn't be late taking their plates away.

This is super. Really super, the best party I've been to for ages, and here I am top of the table with Lindy, all eyes on me. I get complimented on the holly and how clever I was to find it, and fancy it being there behind Kay's husband's works the whole time and him not even noticing it. I get asked about Bruno, I even get asked about details of the Hays of which I've absolutely not the faintest, but I smile anyway and don't let that stop me.

Richard and Kay clear away small plates and refill everybody's glasses. There's a lull.

'Lindy, can I tell my joke? The frog one?'

'Do I know that one, Bruce?'

'It's the one I told when Rebecca came round, when it snowed and Richard stayed, you know, the night we . . .'

'Yes, all right, Bruce, if you must. Hang on. Does

anybody want to hear Bruce's joke? It's clean, it is clean, isn't it, Bruce?'

'Yes, dear, I'm afraid it is.'

Everybody laughs.

'So do you all want to hear Bruce's joke, boys and girls?'

'Oh yes please, Linda,' everybody says in chorus.

Well, she's bloody made me nervous now, hasn't she? And for a second I go blank, can't quite remember how it starts.

'Well, go on then, Bruce.'

'Yes, Lindy. Right. Ahem. Well, there's this chap and he's in a pub . . . Sorry, sorry. Start again.'

Groans all round and shouts of 'Get on with it' from guess who.

'Actually you might like this one, Councillor, it's to do with golf. You play golf, don't you, Councillor?'

'Ah do, lad.'

'Well, there's this chap, er, that's right, he's an oldish sort of chap and he's on a golf course. Anyway, he's just about to take a shot and as he starts on his swing he hears this little squeaky voice.

' "Scuse me," it says. "Excuse me." So the fella stops, and he has a look around but he can't see anything, so he thinks he must've imagined it, or it was the wind or something, so he gets ready to tee off and just as he's about to take a swing he hears the voice again.

' "Excuse me. I'm down here just by your golf trolley. You nearly ran it over me just then." The fella looks down and sitting there in the grass is a frog.

' "Good, you've found me," says the frog. "All you have to do now is give me a kiss. One little kiss and I'll turn into a beautiful princess, I'll marry you and we'll travel the world together in my yacht. I've got a winter palace and houses all over the world and it'll all be yours – a life of luxury, untold riches and a beautiful young wife."

' "Let me get this right," says the fella. "All I have to do is give you one little kiss and you'll turn into a beautiful princess, you'll marry me and we'll travel the world together in your yacht. You've a winter palace and houses all over the world and it'll all be mine – a life of luxury, untold riches and a beautiful young wife. All I have to do now is give you a kiss."

' "That's right," says the frog. "Got it in one."

'The fella straightens up, leans on his club and has a think. He bends down again, scoops up the frog and goes to put it in his pocket.

' "Hang on, hang on just a minute," the frog squeaks. "You're supposed to kiss me."

' "Sorry, love," says the fella. "At my time of life I'd sooner just have a talking frog."'

I've never been so popular. Laughter washes round the table, everybody's faces are shining, the fire's roaring away. Linda beams at me and puts an arm round my shoulder.

'You told that even better than last time, Bruce. Fancy a top-up?'

Richard and Kay bring the turkeys in. Three of the fuckers – one from the Aga, one from our cooker and another from Rebecca's next door. They set them down on the table and there's a round of applause.

Richard pretends to be embarrassed, but you can see he's lapping it up, the smug little cunt. As they ship in all the other grub and dish it out, I feel myself stand.

'Good Friends, good food, good wine, good cheer. Good health, everyone.'

Everybody clinks glasses.

'That was nice, Bruce,' Linda says, helping herself to extra spuds.

'Well, I am nice, Lindy, like you always say, it's nice to be nice. I'm not an idiot and I'm fucking sick of being treated like one all the fucking time.'

Linda tightens her face then turns away. She strikes up a chat with the Vicar.

'Richard, Richard, hey, you, boy, there's a bottle of Scotch in my quarters, cabinet next to the telly. Fetch it down for us, today, if it's all the same to you, sunshine.'

He scuttles off and I hear his footsteps through the ceiling. I turn to the couple from the *Gazette*.

'Just can't get the fucking staff nowadays, can you?' They smile.

'Ah excellent. Here he is now, nice drop of the falling-down water. Have one yourself, sonny, if you think you can hack it.'

'Thanks, Bruce, I will, soon as I've finished in here you and me can stand out the back, take a breath of air and have a drink and a smoke together. OK?'

'For fuck's sake, man, have one with me now. Go

on, one little snifter's not going to hurt you, well, is it now?'

'No. Thanks all the same, Bruce, but I can't now. I'm busy. See you later.'

I turn to my new friends from the *Gazette*, the examiner, the exaggerator, the big gay bumfucker or whatever the fuck it is. Rubbishy little rag anyway, budgie puts on weight, local man lays egg, Christa Ackroyd shaves off her pubes for charity.

'Little ponce. He's not queer though. He looks like a shirtlifter but you should see his girlfriend, cop an eyeful of the tits on that. Blimey. Have that woman washed and brought to my tent.'

They don't say much those two, but they do smile a lot.

May from the Townswomen's Guild is sat next to them all alone. How sad. Tragic. May I? May I fuck. I take her hand.

'On yer tod, May, no husband to hold your hand this Christmas?'

'No, Bruce, he's in hospital.'

'Oh I'm sorry to hear that, May, thought Michael was over his heart attack. Nature's way of telling him to slow down, least that's what Michael said last time I saw him. Never actually thought you could die of smugness, but the way Mike told it, a heart-stopping moment sounded like he'd won a luxury cruise.'

'It's not that, Bruce. It's cancer. Michael's got cancer. Throat cancer.'

'Really? So how's smug St Michael taking that then?

Nature's way of telling him to shut the fuck up by any chance?'

Everybody's finished the main course except me and I really don't fancy any of this stodgy homemade crap any more.

Richard taps me on the shoulder.

'Think we should have that cigarette now, Bruce, get some air.'

'OK, OK, I'm coming, but we'll be requiring the jolly old Jock juice, will we not?'

I reach over to get the bottle and for absolutely no fucking reason half a dozen glasses teeter off the edge of the fucking table.

'Did you see that, Richard? Did you fucking see that? This old dump must be haunted.'

'Come on, Bruce, come outside. Come on, mate.'

I stand and tap my spoon against the bottle. It's greasy, the spoon's all greasy. It slips then skitters away. Like I say, just can't get the staff.

'Can I have your attention please, Ladies and Gentlemen and er, Councillor Stevens. Time for another little joke, I think, same kind of subject style of thing, but even funnier than the last.

'There's a fella walks into a pub, right? And on the bar, on the bar there's a toad, that's right, there's a toad sat on the bar just like that.

' "What's this?" says the fella to the barman – should have mentioned the barman before – anyway it's a pub so there's a bar and behind it there's a barman and on the bar there's this toad. So the fella's just about to tee off and this little squeaky voice says – No. That's not right. So there's this bloke in a pub with a bar and a barman and on the bar there's a toad.

'"What's this?" he says to the barman who's stood behind the bar.

'"It's a toad," says the barman. "But it's a very special toad is this toad and it's made me a lot of money."

'"What's it do?" says the fella. "What's this toad do that makes it so special, what is it this toad that's sat on the bar in this pub that I'm in, what is it that this toad actually does style of thing?" says the fella.

'And the barman, well, the barman that's behind the bar in this pub that the fella's in where there's a toad sat on the bar just like that, that he's asking questions about, the fella, that is, not the toad. Anyway.

'"This," says the barman, "is a cock-sucking toad. Give us five quid and take it in the bogs."

'So the fella gives the barman a fiver, scoops the toad off the counter and goes into the Gents. Five minutes later he's back, big smile on his face.

'"How much you want for this toad?" says the fella to the barman behind the bar of the pub that he's in. "How much for this toad?"

'"Ah well," says the barman, "it's a very special toad is this toad and it's made me a lot of money."

'"Yeah, well," says the fella, "you already said all that. How much for the toad?"

'"Seventy-five quid," says the barman.

'"Done," says the fella.

'So the fella, the fella, right, the fella takes the toad home and when he gets home he goes in the door, he goes in the front door and through to the kitchen and he sets the toad down on the kitchen table.

' "What's this?" says the wife.

' "It's a cock-sucking toad," says the fella.

' "And what am I supposed to do with that?" says the wife.

' "Teach it to cook, then fuck off." '

Sometimes you get quiet and sometimes you get silence.

'We should really go for that cigarette, Bruce,' Richard says. 'Come on now, pal, let's make a move.'

'Happy New Year,' Richard chirps as he lets himself in the back door.

'And to you, Richard,' we say like a pair of idiots.

'Have a good Christmas, Linda, Bruce?'

'Yes,' Linda says. 'Quiet but nice all the same. Did you?'

'Oh yeah, brilliant. Clare came back from Scotland, just put her on the train this morning.'

'And did you?'

'Oh yes, we did, Bruce, and thanks for asking. Lots.'

Lucky little bastard, he's been stuck up to the hilt in that lovely lass all Christmas and I've been stuck here. Linda was right about quiet.

'So what's the sport plan?' Richard asks. 'I know, don't tell me. Look in the black diary.'

'Make yourself a coffee, Richard, I'll fetch the diary and we'll go through it. In fact, you make Richard a coffee, Bruce. Sit yourself down, Richard.'

'Thanks, Linda. Black, please, Bruce.'

I fill the kettle and stick it on – might as well have one myself now I'm officially invisible again.

'You fuck ooffee, Linda?'

'Yes, Bruce, two sugars and don't be so childish, please.'

'That'll teach you,' Richard says.

'What? Teach me what?'

'To filch my material. Anyway, thought you might've eased up on the old comedy after Christmas, made it one of your new year's resolutions. That party really was a once-in-a-lifetime experience.'

Linda comes back with the diary.

'We're closed to visitors till Easter but there's still plenty to be done before then. There's still lot's of cataloguing we haven't got round to, all those tins in the cupboard need sorting and I want you to finish going through the diaries first – you like that, don't you?'

'Yes, I do. You can sit in the warm, for one thing. It's sad reading William's entry when Walter dies though. "My dear brother died today," and then the poem about a tree. Bits of it are quite funny though – they spent most of the war doing PE and watercolours of the local wildlife. I was telling Bruce about my grandad, about him being in the same regiment as William and Walter. I checked with my folks over Christmas but I don't think he ever met them.'

'Well, that's no flipping surprise, is it? Those two kept themselves to themselves, thought they were special, just that little bit different to everybody else even in the middle of a bloody war. They were different all right, they were mad.'

'No, they weren't, Bruce,' Linda snaps, 'they were

just different. They were special, and if they hadn't've been I'd not have a job here, and we'd not have a house. Anyway, would you please not interrupt while I'm talking to Richard.'

'Actually, Linda, I have to agree with Bruce on that one. I've been thinking about it over Christmas, I've been thinking about it a lot, and I reckon they were a bit barmy.'

'How do mean?'

'Well, think about it, it's classic really, isn't it? Somebody dies and you keep their room just the same, loads of people do that, my gran did, always set a place for my grandad, a way of dealing with it, diverting grief into objects or whatever, but these two took it to extremes, lived on the surface of the house like that irritating man says in the video, didn't change anything for the next forty years. I mean, I know it's good for us, the Trust and everything, but it's not exactly normal behaviour, is it?'

'I think they were poofs, bloody fart-catchers, the pair of 'em.'

'Bruce, will you not . . .'

'That crossed my mind too, actually, but I don't think they were, er, gay, especially not William. If you read his diaries and then look at his cash books I reckon something was going on.'

'Like what, Richard?' Linda stirs her coffee, blows on her coffee, then sips her coffee and looks worried.

'Well, like I say. William kept accounts down to every last penny, every last farthing, right? As you know he also kept a diary, routine stuff around the house, books he read, walks he took, birds he spotted.'

'Feathered ones anyway.'

'Yes, very funny, Bruce, but the odd thing is that one day the maid, Beatrice I think her name was, who'd been at the Hays for ever, just disappears. She stops getting mentioned in the diary at all and the same week – and this is the bit that got me suspicious – the same week Beatrice leaves, she stops getting paid, which is what you'd expect, but there's a hundred quid drawn out of the bank and marked paid in William's cashbook – which is a hell of a lot of money. He doesn't record what it's for then and he never does after.'

'So?

'So maybe and this is only a maybe, maybe William paid her off, maybe he got her pregnant and then sent her away somewhere to have the kid, if there was a kid, and I'm just babbling now – but it's a thought, isn't it?'

Linda clears her throat and opens the diary.

'Well, that's all very interesting, Richard, and I'm sure there's a perfectly logical explanation . . .'

'There's a logical explanation all right, my darling wife. William laid his hose in the housemaid's Doris, she joined the club, he paid her to sod off. If there was any other explanation William would have put it in the bloody cashbook. Not going to look too cosy in our guidebook that, is it? "Welcome to the Hays where traditional shagging occurred." Shall I ring Simon now and tell him, get it printed up before the new season opens? Wonder where they did it. We could have a plaque, or several plaques, get the Friends to fundraise for them. "On this very spot William inserted his old-fashioned Edwardian etcetera, etcetera." '

'That's enough, Bruce!'

I can see Richard's trying very hard not to, but he fails and breaks out laughing.

'Shock horror,' he giggles, 'budgie puts on weight, local man lays egg, people used to do it in the old days. So it wasn't invented in the '60s after all.'

'Look,' Linda says, 'can we just drop this. It's not, it's not appropriate.'

'What's that mean, Linda? If you mean politically correct, forget it. You, me and Bruce can talk about shagging all morning if we like, so long as we use the proper terms.'

'It means, Richard, that I do not want to talk about it, and on no account are you to mention this to anyone either, and I mean anyone. I did hear a similar story myself when I first started here, but can we just leave it. Please.

'Anyway, Richard, so what I was going to say, if you'd just let me get a word in, is that one of the things we have to do before the Hays House opens in April is to find you a job.'

'Eh? I don't want a job, I mean I've got a job here and anyway you said . . .'

'About you having the house? Yes, I know I did, and I still think it's a good idea.'

'Well, that's a flipping relief, but I don't get it. Why do I need a job if I'm working here?'

So Linda tells him, and it's the first I've heard of it but as I say, Linda never tells me anything. Apparently Simon from the Trust phoned on Christmas Eve, Christmas fucking Eve, would you believe, for a progress report on Richard. Linda praised him to the skies and Simon said there was a position going at a place called Willow Road down in London – flat of some artist or designer, Arnie Goldfinger, who I've certainly never heard of – which needed temporary cover while the real custodian was on maternity leave, which is pretty funny considering the conversation we've just had. He said that it'd be a fantastic opportunity, although I'm prepared to bet Simon said farntarstic opportunity for Richard to prove himself before he applied for the job at the Hays.

'Well, I wouldn't trust that stuck-up . . .'

'Bruce. So what do you think, Richard?'

'Well, I have to agree with you again there, Bruce. Anybody who uses a beard trimmer that carefully's definitely not to be believed, but blimey, Linda, I've only been back an hour and you're getting rid of me. I'll do it though – if you think you can manage here without me.'

Linda smiles.

'I knew you would and I expect we'll struggle along somehow without you, won't we, Bruce? But it won't be till the new season anyway and it's not even definite either. You'll have to apply for the job and you'll need a really good reference.'

'Which you'll give me?'

'Yes, if you can possibly manage to stop acting giddy for five minutes, and I'll help with your application too.'

Richard grins at me.

'Looks like you'll be finally getting to see the back of me then, eh, Bruce? What with Linda's brains and my looks, try not to take it too hard though, mate, let's try to make the most of our last four precious months together and promise me you'll write. Wonderful thing is maternity, appropriate or not.'

Richard stands and heads for the office.

'Right,' he says, 'missing you already, Brucie, so let's see what else I can turn up from these 'ere diaries, laudanum, jazz mags, naked photos of Queen Victoria, electric guitars, banger racing?'

He slams the office door. Linda smiles. I smile back. We hear him singing.

' "Dah dee dah dee dah, dah, dah, all my brain and body need, very good indeed." '

'He's not calmed down over Christmas, has he, Bruce, not one tiny bit?'

'No, dear, he's got worse.'

Richard'll get that job all right. He'll piss it. He's young, he's got bags of energy and a lovely lass to keep him warm at night and tell him he'll do fine. And I will miss him, I really will, another bloke. God forgive me for saying this about the little ponce, but I really don't want him to go. Another bloke, a man who understands what it's like for me here and makes it OK, helps Lindy to cope with me and me to cope with Lindy.

He's a nice lad is Richard, a really nice lad.

Linda's at the fang snatcher this morning for a scale and polish and I'm on a gypsy's warning.

Told me off in advance she did. Hold the fort till I get back. Don't do anything daft. I look at the bottle on the table. The little brown bottle with the child-proof cap, the little brown bottle that calibrates my life, gets me up in the mornings, controls the way I act, controls my whole useless life, and I think fuck that.

Richard was in here yesterday and he saw them, the pills.

'Jesus, Bruce, I'd have killed for these when I was a student, specially round exam time,' he said.

'These pills?' I said.

'Yeah, those pills. Three of them and you're flying. I've heard you, mate, asking Linda if I'm on drugs, and it turns out it's you.'

'What?'

'Do you not know what these are?'

'No, not really.'

'These are dexies, mate, Dexedrine, speed – you know, what the mods used to take, and the northern soul boys – you know, the ones with the baggy trousers.

Don't need the baggy pants though, pop a few of these and nothing, nothing will happen down there. You really shouldn't drink either. Did you know that?'

'No. Yes.'

So these aren't for dancing, putting on your best Fred Perry, doing the Monkey Spanner?'

'No. You've lost me there.'

'Were you hatched middle-aged, Bruce, born wearing a cravat?'

'No, no, we lived in a village. We moved from a small town to a village. I drew pictures, I read books, went fishing almost every day. When I was young.'

'Well, anyway, Bruce, these here are dexies, you know, like in Dexy's Midnight Runners, "Come on, Eileen"?'

'Is that, is that like a sex thing? I only ever met one girl who'd let me do that and then only the once. She was drunk and next day she said I was a pig.'

'No, Bruce, and thanks for sharing that. It's a song, just a song.'

Anyway, fuck them. I don't need them, little white dots three times daily, ruining my life. I'm fine. Lindy's fine, Richard's fine. Bruno's fine, everything's fine. Splendid even.

So I don't take them. I don't take Bruno out either. I shut the back gate and let him into the garden. If he shits, he shits. I'll clear it later. I leave the back door open a crack, I don't wash and I don't shave.

Me? I'm going to take it easy this morning. I make

myself a pot of tea, put it on a tray – milk, sugar, packet of biscuits – and climb the stairs to my room.

I kick off my slippers, feel the soft thick carpet sprouting up between my toes and lie down on the bed. I take my book from the bedside table.

The Secret War, four books in one: *The Man Who Never Was*, *The White Rabbit*, *Ill Met By Moonlight*, *Carve Her Name With Pride*.

'This volume brings together four impressive true stories of the Second World War,' it says on the back cover. 'Complete and unabridged.'

Before I open at the red-leather bookmark halfway through *The Man Who Never Was*, I turn back the cover and read what Lindy wrote. Fountain pen, royal-blue Quink, girlish joined-up handwriting.

To my Darling Bruce, I hope you have a lovely Xmas. Lots of Love Linda XXX.

I wake with a dry mouth and the old guts are on hot wash. It's nearly half-eleven and there's a fair amount of noise coming from next door.

They've got a radio in there and they're laughing. It isn't allowed. A radio is not allowed in there. William wrote in his diary, 'I Will Not Have The Blaring Of Saxophones In My House,' and sent his brother into town with his tail between his legs and back to the shop where he bought the radio. They fell out about that. Walter says so in his diary. He only wanted one for the cricket. Radios are not allowed.

I go to the top of the attic stairs, across the landing, and open the connecting door to the Hays.

'Who's down there?'

'Me an' Richard,' Kay shouts. 'We're getting the parents' bedroom ready for opening next week – we'll be round for coffee in a bit.'

'Turn that radio off now.'

'Why?'

'They're not allowed, you both know that. Turn it off.'

'Linda said it was OK, said so long as we didn't play music it was all right.'

'It is not. Radios are not allowed.'

'Oh fuck off, Bruce.'

I snap the door to and go downstairs to the kitchen, our kitchen, mine and Lindy's kitchen, in our house where we live. The house that's overrun with do-gooders and smart-arses, the house where I have no say, no sex and no feelings. My mouth's so dry I can hardly speak, my tongue's stiff and I feel a bit dizzy. I make myself a coffee, smoke a fag and wash my face in the sink.

I go to call Bruno from the garden. The back door's locked.

Up the stairs, top landing, open connecting door.

'Right. Who locked the back door?'

'I did, Bruce,' Richard calls back. 'Anybody could have walked in and there's no need to shout.'

'Where are the keys?'

'On the kitchen table, Bruce, where I found them when I walked in.'

'You walked in, just waltzed into my house without telling me? How dare you. Just who the hell do you think you are?'

'No, I knocked for ages, then I put my head round the door and shouted, then I went in. I thought you'd gone out. Sorry.'

'If you ever, ever, do that again, young man, I will punch your fucking head. Linda's away this morning. She left me in charge. When Linda's away you report to me. You will report to me.'

I slam the connecting door and go downstairs.

Five minutes later Richard's in the kitchen all smiles.

'You were joking just then, Bruce – about punching my fucking head?'

I misjudged the first slightly and it caught him in the throat. The second and the third were placed much better and, as he bounced off the cellar door and fell back against the work-top, I could see in his eyes that Richard knew just how much I was enjoying this.

'Kay's off sick and Richard says he won't be coming back. I was just on the phone to him and do you know he swore at me, said the f word.'

'Did he now, Lindy?'

'Yes, Bruce, when I told him he'd have had to have put up with a lot worse in the army – like you said. He said he didn't join the fucking army and then he put the phone down. You did only shout at him, Bruce?'

'Yes of course, dear. Why?'

'He seemed really upset, you two've had words before, but he's never sworn at me.'

'He was always swearing, you just never noticed before. Soon as we met him he said fuck.'

'Did he?'

' "Thank fuck for that," he said, when you said it was all right to smoke. You just never noticed.'

'Well, he's let us down this time, it just doesn't seem like him. Are you sure, do you promise me, Bruce, that nothing else happened?'

'Yes. I mean no, nothing else happened.'

'You shouldn't have shouted at him and it is funny that you didn't hear him knocking.'

'I was busy. I was, I was vacuuming, yes, that's it, I

was vacuuming so that's why I didn't hear him. You left me in charge and he should have reported to me.'

'Actually, Bruce, Richard did do the right thing. He reported to Kay who's a Trust employee when you're not and he locked the door behind him. He should've let you know he was here though.'

'Well, he didn't.'

'Bruce, you do promise me you didn't do anything silly?'

'Linda, how many times. I shouted at him. I know I shouldn't have but that's all and I'm sorry. What will you do anyway, about Richard getting the Hays, that job at Willow Road?'

'I don't know, I'm not sure yet. I don't know, Bruce, but if he gets Willow Road he'll be in with a very good chance for this place when we leave. The sooner the better for that I think.'

The letter came a week later. His application for Willow Road and a letter. A handwritten, really nice, chatty letter. Linda cried when she read it.

Richard thanked her for all her help, said she was the kindest, most generous person he'd ever worked with, had the pleasure of working with, apologised for leaving at such short notice, and wished me well. He said I could keep his books and said he'd prefer not to work in an environment where he felt threatened and completely failed to mention the fact I'd battered him three times round the kitchen, split his lip and made his nose bleed.

He wished me well. The little cunt wished me well.

We've a new volunteer started, decent set of tits, no brain, face like a pizza. Put a bag over it and I suppose it'd be OK though. Richard's been on the phone to Lindy quite a bit, the application for Willow Road's done, dusted and posted. She's agreed to be a referee and he's still not shopped me. He won't now, I feel sure of it. There'll never be another one like him.

The man who never was.

Pottering around the old homestead.

You know that feeling.

You're on a four-day pass and you're sat on on a train in the railway station, watching the clock and waiting. You sit there nursing a hard-on for your wife, sweetheart, sister or whatever, and you've read their last letter so many times that you already know it by heart, but you fish it out and read it anyway.

Only you don't really read it, you don't read the words, your eye just flicks across pages folded and refolded so many times they look like maps and it follows the shapes the ink makes on the page.

You're so bored and sick with no breakfast and too many fags, your stomach heaves if you even think about eating the chocolate or the fruit you've got for them, just for something to do. Then the train alongside you pulls away but it feels like you that's moving.

I stare out of the kitchen window and the clouds are whipping across east to west. I fix on the clouds and, as I stop them with my eye, the green lawn and the black-soil flowerbeds slip off east. The bin and the bunker lean towards town, the fence blurs then disappears.

The phone goes.

Lindy's out. Pizza face is with a group of visitors.

'Hello, Hays.' Best Telephone Voice.

'Hello, may I speak to the custodian?' Posh Trust Bitch.

'Speaking.'

'Oh hello, just checking on your long-term volunteer's reference for the Willow Road posting. It's a very strong application but there's stiff competition and I was just wondering, is there anything you'd like to add on an informal basis?'

'Yes, I'm afraid there is.'

'Yes?'

'Yes. I'm sorry to say we've, I've, only just had it brought to my attention that Richard has a criminal record, a string of convictions as long as your arm. Drugs, fraud, theft. Terrible things.'

'Really?'

'Yes. I'm afraid he's not to be trusted.'

We sit separately in the evenings.

Linda has her sewing and the telly. I like to read or listen to the wireless. I fill a mug with water from the kitchen tap, wash down the last of today's tablets and fetch my book from the shelf where Linda keeps the cookery books, some film-processing envelopes and the latest Innovations Catalogue.

There's always a bit of a nasty moment as the tablets take hold, a rush of useless energy and a misplaced feeling of hope. I lay the book down on the table, make a deliberate effort to stay calm then fold it open and remove the scarlet Hays House bookmark which Linda made me pay for.

I smooth it on to the table, run my fingers along its hard-glazed surface and around the gold embossing, then I turn it over and smooth out the soft suede.

It's no use though, I can't settle. I fetch the garage key from the back of the cellar door, pick up the car keys off the side by the kettle and go out into the dusk and into the car park. The days are getting longer, the nights are getting shorter. It won't be long now, it won't be long till summer comes.

I twist the key marked Squire into the lock marked

Squire, open the garage doors then drag them to behind me. Our little car. I undo the driver's door, slide into her and turn on the radio.

Heavenly shades of night are falling, it's twilight time.
Out of the mist your voice is calling, 'tis twilight time.
When purple-coloured curtains mark the end of day
I'll hear you, my dear, at twilight time.

Deepening shadows gather splendour as day is done
Fingers of night will soon surrender the setting sun
I count the moments, darling, till you're here with me
Together at last at twilight time.

Here, in the afterglow of day, we keep our
    rendezvous beneath the blue
And, in the same old sweet way, I fall in love as
    I did then.

Deep in the dark your kiss will thrill me like days
    of old
Lighting the spark of love that fills me with dreams
    untold
Each day I pray for evening just to be with you
Together at last at twilight time
Together at last at twilight time.

I wind down all the window and turn the key in the ignition. The engine starts up, sweet as a nut. It won't be long now, it won't be long.

The sun's belting through the curtains. I lie in my bed looking at all my best drawings pinned around the walls. There's a really big one of an avocet – which is my favourite – and next to it a half-finished drawing of a sailing dinghy.

Mum calls me from downstairs. Breakfast's almost ready.

I don't want to go to school today. I'd much rather just go fishing. It's such a nice day.

Mum calls me again. Breakfast's ready. Then I remember. It's the first day of the summer holidays and they stretch out in front of me like one enormous yes.

Me and Ian Roper have got longer than anybody else.

I pull back the curtains. The sunshine crashes in and swamps my room. This morning I'm helping Dad respray the Hillman. He says he'll do my bike as well. This afternoon I'm going fishing.

A Note on the Author

Born in Leicestershire, Simon Crump studied philosophy at Sheffield University and has lived in Sheffield for the last twenty years. His short stories have appeared in numerous magazines and anthologies, and he is the author of the short-story collections *My Elvis Blackout* and *Monkey's Birthday*. *Twilight Time* is his first novel.